Shadows of the

Heart

A Bindarra Creek Romance

Lee Christine

Shadows of the Heart
Copyright © 2015 Lee Christine
All rights reserved
Lee Christine
ISBN: 978-0-9944256-1-4

DEDICATION

To my amazing children, Danielle & Adam – I am so proud of you, you never cease to amaze me!

ACKNOWLEDGMENTS

To my ever supportive and steadfast husband, Damian. I couldn't do this without you.

To my wonderful mother, Bonnie. You are the greatest!

To my critique partners, Anna Clifton and Linda Hills for your wise counsel.

To Craig Parish for taking the time to explain to me everything I needed to know about split rail fences, Angus cattle, Herefords, Brahman and planting seasonal feeds.

To Rebekah Turner for the amazing cover design for Shadows of the Heart.

A special thank you to my fellow members of the Bindarra Creek Romance series – it's been a huge amount of fun. We've shared lots of laughs and good times. Thank you sincerely for all your hard work and support.

A Bindarra Creek Romance

Drama, intrigue, suspense, adventure and honest, country goodness – welcome to Bindarra Creek where life and love in a small country town has never been more challenging.

LEE CHRISTINE

CHAPTER ONE

Cameron Reid eased his foot off the accelerator and stared at the signpost illuminated in the sweep of headlights.

'*Welcome to Bindarra Creek. We are a tidy town.*'

Turning down Holst's Planets Suite on Classic FM, he slowed the car, lowered the driver's window and propped his elbow on the sill. A bracing, pre-dawn breeze rushed into the cabin carrying the scent of pine and eucalypt. With a grimace, he repositioned his stiff, left leg and dragged in one deep breath after another. If anything could expunge the five-year build-up of Middle Eastern dust lining his lungs, it was the untainted air of the northern tablelands.

One hand working the wheel, he drove along Mt. Ingalls Road. At five in the morning his home town was shrouded in a heavy cloud of fog, the only sign of life a narrow column of light shining from the window of the local fire station. Hopefully, the cool change that had swept across the ranges would bring rain and lower the fire danger rating. Since leaving the green hills of the Hunter Valley, the countryside had steadily been turning browner.

Two blocks further on, Cameron glanced towards Main Street and the historic part of town; the bank, the post office, the line of two storey timber shops with their suspended wooden awnings. He smiled a little as he glimpsed the cinema where he'd worked as a teenager, serving popcorn and choc tops and chatting up the girls while he sold them a ticket.

Slowing the car to a crawl, he approached the roundabout, the stone cenotaph in the centre a sobering reminder of past soldiers who hadn't made it back. He slid his elbow along the sill and raised his hand in a solemn salute. He was one of the lucky ones. He'd made it home, returned to the land, to his roots.

One thing was for sure, he'd never leave again.

He yawned, eyes gritty, quadriceps aching from where the army surgeon had dug out a piece of shrapnel the size of a golf ball. So much for his decision to press on through the night. He should have dossed down in one of the country motels along the way, but eagerness to see his father and sister had spurred him on.

Cameron squinted at the road, the glare from the low beam reflecting off the fog and back through the windscreen. He reached over and turned up the demister, wishing the rented Toyota was fitted with fog lights. But it wasn't far now. Only fifteen minutes until he reached Bindarra Downs.

A flash from the pavement had him standing on the brakes, heart leaping, hands tightening on the wheel. Blood, dismembered body parts and flying pieces of molten metal filled his mind's eye as he gritted his teeth and braced for the explosion.

But there was nothing.

No deafening bomb blast.

No night fire from war guns.

Just the swish of wipers over the low hum of Classic FM. And his heartbeat, outpacing the seconds flashing on the digital clock.

Cameron blinked hard and shook his head at the years of conditioning that had him acting on instinct. This wasn't a combat zone. This was Bindarra Creek, and the dark figure standing on the curb wasn't an enemy lurking by the roadside, but an early morning jogger.

As his heart continued to race he raised a hand, not in apology, more an indication that the jogger should cross.

She came slowly at first, his gaze following the flare of her hips and shapely curve of long, slender legs. She wore running skins and a tracksuit top, her hair covered by the hood. As she stepped into the full beam of headlights she removed her earbuds and turned to look right at him, like she was expecting him to lean out the window and say something.

He gave a slight nod and twisted his lips into a semblance of a smile. She didn't return the greeting, just stared at him as she crossed the road, eyes two dark pools in a pale, delicately shaped face.

Cameron blew out a relieved breath as she headed for the opposite curb. The flash that had brought out the soldier in him had been nothing more than the in-built reflectors in the trainers she wore.

Uneasy at the way the woman had stared at him, like he was trouble, he pulled away and continued to watch her in his side mirror. Twice she turned and looked over her shoulder as though he might do a U-turn and come after her. Then she began to run. A moment later she disappeared into the fog.

Cameron relaxed his jaw in an effort to let go of the tension. He drove through the outskirts of town without seeing another person. Fifteen minutes later, just as the first rays of sunshine lightened the horizon he sighted the white split rail fence that bordered Bindarra Downs.

He swallowed the rising lump in his throat and turned into the driveway, steering wheel vibrating in his hands as the tyres hit the cattle grid. Normally the black, wrought iron gates would be closed at this time. Today, they stood open like familiar arms waiting to embrace him. Waiting to welcome him home.

CHAPTER TWO

Adrenaline charged into Rhiannon's system like high octane fuel, sharpening her senses and lengthening her stride. She glanced over her shoulder, but there was no sign of the car that had screeched to a halt more than ten minutes ago in the middle of Mt. Ingalls Road.

Computing an alternate route in her head, she weaved her way through the back streets, a mixture of residential dwellings and light industrial factories. Could the driver be the stranger she'd noticed in town last week, the man who'd been sitting in the front window of the Cyprus coffee shop? He'd taken a long, hard look at her when she'd popped in to have her morning coffee, made her so uneasy she'd changed her order to a takeaway. She'd run into him again later in the week, buying a paper at the newsagents.

Rhiannon shivered inside her damp running gear. According to the large Avis sticker visible in the top right corner of the windscreen, the car was a rental, from

Sydney. Still, there was no way of knowing if the driver was the man she'd seen about town. Only the lower half of his face had been visible.

A dog barked and she jumped, nerve endings tingling all the way to her extremities. She shied away from the fence as a light came on. A door opened. A man shouted at the dog. Only then did she remember the earbuds clutched in her hand, hear the tinny clash of symbols over the rhythmic tread of her footfalls.

Rhiannon slipped between two parked cars and crossed the street near the boarded up butter factory. Was she overreacting? Possibly. The driver with the square cut jaw could have been passing through town enroute to Armidale. But why stop so suddenly in the middle of the main drag when she hadn't been anywhere near a pedestrian crossing?

She ran on, blowing clouds of mist into the air like a fire breathing dragon. Normally, the early morning dark wrapped around her like a protective cloak, shielding her from the unwanted attention a boot camp or gym class might bring. Attention she'd been advised to avoid.

But not this morning. This morning she'd been exposed in the full glare of a stranger's headlights.

Another two turns and her street sign materialised ahead like the beacon of a lighthouse. Moments later she was on the front porch, pulling off her trainers without bothering to undo the laces. She opened the solid hardwood front door, painted in a federation green colour, and let herself in. Warm air from the oil heater hit the exposed flesh of her face and lower legs.

Comforting sounds came from the kitchen out back, the hiss of a kettle, the clink of cutlery on china.

Mrs. Bannister, preparing the first cuppa of the day.

Rhiannon turned and engaged the deadlock. She couldn't afford to become complacent just because the defendant's lawyers had left her alone for twelve months. Not with the court case due to be heard in six weeks.

An image of Doctor Dominic Mullen formed in her mind and Rhiannon's stomach twisted into a sickening knot. To this day, the man strutted the wards of the Royal Mercy Hospital like God himself while she'd been made a pariah, forced to leave her family, her friends and the city she loved, forced to take a job in a country town.

But Dr. Mullen was scared, and desperate enough to have sent someone to Bindarra Creek before to 'encourage' her to drop the defamation proceedings she'd taken against him.

Looping the cord of her music player around unsteady fingers, Rhiannon padded around the Edwardian style furniture. At the window, she peered at the street through the gap in the lacy curtains. She'd long familiarised herself with the neighbour's daily comings and goings.

The plumber's ute was parked across the road and further along she could just make out the shape of the caravan belonging to the retired couple a few doors down. Next door, in the driveway of a house rented by an indeterminate number of backpackers, stood a wheelie bin with its lid open, overflowing with empty bottles, pizza boxes and beer cartons.

Rhiannon smiled a little. The backpackers were harmless, the house 'party central'. They stayed for a few weeks or months, picking up casual work on the properties in the area, nothing to worry about apart from whether the budget would stretch to cover the cost of the next party.

'I thought I heard you come in.'

Rhiannon spun around to see Mavis Bannister, or May as the locals called her, standing in the doorway, silver hair set in blue curlers, stout figure swathed in a soft pink dressing gown.

'What are you looking at?' May asked.

Rhiannon let the curtain fall back into place and yanked the hood back from her sweaty forehead. 'A car stopped for me. It really creeped me out. It was travelling slowly along Mr. Ingalls Road like it was looking for something, or *someone*. A rental, from Sydney. When the driver saw me he screeched to a halt. Then he just sat there, watching while I crossed.'

For a few moments May just looked at her. Then she came further into the room, the hem of her dressing gown swishing on the carpet.

'Oh lovey ... don't you go jumping to conclusions that he was looking for you in particular. It's probably just some weirdo. You can never be too careful. Criminals are everywhere these days.'

'Not really, May.' Rhiannon smiled a little and slid her iPod into her tracksuit pocket. 'Crime rates have remained pretty steady for a long time. There's an illusion things are worse because of the saturated media coverage we're exposed to.'

May gave one of her unconvinced snorts, the kind that said you could talk until you were blue in the face but it wouldn't change her mind. 'I don't like you running around the streets in the dark, full stop. From the minute you leave the house, I can't go back to sleep. That's why I get up and busy myself getting the tea ready for when you come home.'

Rhiannon closed the distance between them and took hold of the older woman's hand. How grateful she was that May had advertised for a boarder the same week Rhiannon had been offered the position of Bindarra Creek's home nurse. 'I don't mean to worry you, but it's the only time I get to exercise.'

May's misshapen, arthritic fingers tightened around Rhiannon's. 'I know you're busy, and Lord only knows what we're going to do around here when it's time for you to go back to the city.'

It was the first time May had raised the subject of Rhiannon's impending departure, and now, as she gazed into the older woman's bright blue eyes the thought of saying goodbye to May and the other locals filled Rhiannon with a deep sadness.

'I've loved my time in Bindarra Creek. And it's not over yet. I have another six weeks.'

'That'll go quickly but we'll not talk of it now.' May squared her shoulders. 'Let's go into the kitchen and you can tell me what make of car it was over a cup of tea. We can keep an eye out for it in town today.'

Rhiannon's lips twitched. She'd always found May's love of small town amateur sleuthing more amusing than her firm belief there was no problem a nice hot cup of tea couldn't fix.

'Did you bring in the milk?'

Milk?

She'd been in such a hurry to get inside she must have missed it. 'I didn't see it on the verandah.'

'Go on!' May waved a hand towards the kitchen. 'I'll get it.'

Rhiannon didn't move, grimacing as her landlady tried opening the front door.

'We're back to locking up are we?' May clicked her tongue against the roof of her mouth as she disengaged the deadlock. 'You really did get a fright this morning. I must remember to start carrying the house keys with me again.'

Rhiannon headed down the wide hallway complete with 1970's blue flowered wallpaper. How many times had she locked up in the early days only for May to come home and not be able to get into her house? Too many to count.

In the kitchen, she slipped off her track top and hung it over the back of a chair, cheered by the cosy warmth of the room. Lifting the heavy teapot with its multi-coloured crocheted tea-cosy, Rhiannon poured two cups of tea and thought about the first time she'd met May.

'Mr. Bannister died years ago,' May had explained as she'd given Rhiannon a tour through the neat-as-a-pin house and attached granny flat. 'My granddaughter recently graduated from the New England University. She used to spend a lot of weekends here. I miss the company now she's gone.'

She'd leaned forward and stared at Rhiannon, blue eyes twinkling. 'You kids are good for us oldies. You keep us young.'

Rhiannon smiled at the memory and sat down at the solid mahogany table. At thirty, it had been a long time since anyone had called her a 'kid'.

She turned as May came into the kitchen.

'The milk's not there.' The older woman opened a cupboard and took down a carton of long life milk, eyeing it with a suspicion she usually reserved for supermarket bought pastry. 'I always knew this stuff would come in handy one day.'

'Maybe his truck wouldn't start.' Rhiannon took the milk from May, opened the carton and added a dash to their tea. The arthritis in May's fingers was getting worse, making it difficult for her not only to open cartons, but open jars and turn the taps on and off too. 'You still taking those glucosamine tablets I got you?'

'Yes, nurse. They're extra stiff in the morning, that's all. Now, what was the make of that car you're all worked up about?'

Rhiannon told her it was a Toyota and for the next few minutes they drank their tea in silence.

'I don't trust Dominic Mullen's legal team.' Rhiannon said eventually. 'What's to stop them sending someone up here to lean on me again?'

'Because they tried that once before and you were adamant you wouldn't drop the defamation charges.'

'Not unless he signs a Statutory Declaration clearing my name. That will help with my application for unfair dismissal.' Rhiannon stood and carried her empty cup to the sink. 'Maybe I'm just on edge because the hearing date's getting close.'

'It's understandable, the man destroyed your career. But don't you worry, I'll keep a look out for the car and this man you're speaking of. And I'll ask the other Country Women's Association ladies, someone's sure to know who he is.'

'Thanks May.'

'So, what's on today?' May asked in an obvious effort to change the subject.

'I promised Doc. Warner I'd take another run out to the Reid property—try and speak to Jed.

'Oh. I hope you have better luck this time.'

'Me too.' For many people, visiting one of the area's most historic and picturesque grazing properties would be regarded as a privilege rather than a chore. But not for Rhiannon. Last time she'd gone out to Bindarra Downs, Jed Reid had sent her packing with a firm directive not to come back.

'I can understand Doc. Warner sending you in his place lovey. Jed's a personal friend of his. It must be hard for him to see Jed the way he is now.'

Rhiannon thought about May's comments as she headed for the shower. Doc. Warner was a man who cared for the community, cared for his friends and rarely took holidays because the town couldn't get another doctor to cover for him. His life was one of dedication and devotion.

And this morning she would do everything in her power to help him by convincing Gerard Reid to relinquish his license.

CHAPTER THREE

The fences needed painting and his mother's beloved garden beds in the centre of the circular driveway lay neglected and overgrown. The sandstone fountain had long been turned off, a casualty of the ongoing drought.

Cameron's heart missed a beat when he spotted his mother's favourite rose bush, the one his father had given her on Mother's Day years ago. He couldn't remember its name, but the rose had thrived under his mother's loving care. Now, it looked forlorn, thin and scraggly.

Cameron threw the Toyota into park, killed the engine and opened the door.

Cosmetic things.

How he wished everything could be so easily fixed.

He was levering his stiff body from the driver's seat when the homestead's screen door flew open, the wooden frame crashing against the bricks with a familiarity reminiscent of his childhood. A slight figure raced headlong down the steps and across the gravel driveway.

'Cam! I can't believe you're finally home.'

The relief in Victoria's choked out words caused a lump of suppressed emotion to rise once again in Cameron's throat. Fearing his gammy leg would give way, he gripped the doorframe as his sister launched herself at him. He managed to catch her and stay upright, pulling her to him in a one-arm bear hug and uttering the words he knew she needed to hear.

'I'm home for good now Tori, I promise.'

She nodded, face buried in the soft cotton of his tee-shirt, arms tight around his waist.

He leaned down and kissed the top of her head and though he murmured the words 'Come on, midget, don't cry', he kept his arm around her while she did. The fourteen-year age difference had somehow made them closer, though Victoria hadn't always been thrilled with it, on many occasions accusing him of acting like a second father.

After a while she loosened her hold and stepped back. 'They're happy tears, Cam.'

'Just as well.' He ruffled her curly hair the way he always had and curved his lips into a reassuring smile. 'Stop worrying. This is a good day.'

A movement on the verandah caught his eye. Jed Reid was standing at the top of the steps. Thinner, his stoop more acute than when Cameron had last seen him, his right hand was tucked into a trouser pocket in an effort to disguise the Parkinson's shake.

Cameron walked to the bottom of the steps and looked up at the man who until the age of eighteen had taught him everything there was to know about the importance of family and the land. *'Dad!'*

Jed's eyes glistened at the husky greeting though his attempt at a smile failed to soften the mask like expression. 'Welcome home, mate. I'd come down there but you'd only have to get me back up again.'

Overwhelmed with relief that he'd finally made it home, Cameron ascended the stairs as quickly as his injured leg would allow. Moments later, he stepped into his father's embrace, still surprisingly strong despite his debilitated body.

'No-one knows you're back.' Tori said later as they sat around the kitchen table. 'Dad refused to tell anyone in case he jinxed you.'

'Fair enough. The last thing I want is a welcoming party.'

Tori frowned. 'It seems kind of rude not to let our friends and neighbours know, you being the town hero and all.'

'I'm no hero, and they'll hear soon enough.' News swept through Bindarra Creek like an out of control bushfire. Nothing surer, one of the locals would take it upon themselves to organise a welcome home party. *Christ,* he couldn't think of anything worse than having to rock up at the local bowlo and make small talk while the locals toasted him. All he wanted was to stay put, whip the property into shape and have some serious conversations with his father about his health.

'How's the place withstanding the drought?' he asked, wondering how long he could lie low before the locals got wind of his arrival.

'Better than most.' Jed's cup clattered into the saucer. 'There's plenty of feed in the far paddocks. The herd's there now, close by Angus McGregor's property.'

McGregor was a good man and Cameron would always be grateful for the help he'd afforded Jed. He had no problem letting McGregor know he was back. 'When were they last checked?'

'A week ago, maybe.'

Cameron smiled. 'Then that's first on my list tomorrow.'

'Don't be too hasty to get back to work, that leg still looks bad.'

Typical of his father to be more worried about his son's leg than his own degenerative condition. 'I'll take the quad. It'll be a while before I'm comfortable on a bike.'

'I can't wait to see all the girls in town showering you with sympathy.' Tori smirked at him over the rim of her mug and spoke in a high pitched voice. 'Can I help you Cam, can I rub your leg?'

Cameron cocked his head at Jed. 'This, from a sixteen year old who drinks Milo from a Winnie the Pooh mug.'

They all laughed and Cameron was pleased the family dynamic remained unchanged. He'd been surprised from discussions he'd had with the men under his command how some families were unable to co-exist under the same roof once the children reached adulthood. That had never been the case with the Reids. Three generations had worked the land and happily co-habited in this very homestead.

Cameron studied the faces of his family, revelling in the sight of them. Both were older, changed somewhat, and yet comfortingly familiar. Listening to his men griping and whining about their families only made him realise how lucky he was. It was at those times he'd suffered his worst bouts of homesickness. Keeping in touch with his family had helped, speaking to them every week on Skype when possible. Just general news. They appreciated he couldn't talk about the special ops stuff.

'We should have some kind of celebration, even if it's just us,' Tori grumbled.

'Maybe Dad will let you take the day off school today.'

His sister shook her head, irrepressible curls bouncing all over the place. 'I don't think that's a good idea.'

Surprised, he eyed his sister. The Tori he knew was like any regular teenager, more than willing to accept a day off school if given the chance.

'Why? Are you behind?' He'd have to arrange a tutor if she was struggling.

Before she could answer, the rev of a car engine coming up the driveway made him look up. 'Are you expecting anyone?'

Jed shook his head. 'Not me.'

Tori was on her feet before Cameron could stand. 'Stay there, I'll go.'

A minute later she was back. 'It's the nurse.'

Jed groaned.

'What nurse?' asked Cameron.

'Blasted woman! Tell her my son's home and we haven't even unpacked the car.'

'The community nurse calls in from time to time.' Tori looked pointedly at Cameron though she spoke with a forced patience he suspected was directed at their father. 'She's really nice.'

'She's a pain in the arse!'

Cameron stood up. 'Okay. Tori, go and get dressed for school, I'll speak to her.' It was time he started taking the load off his sister, time for Tori to be a normal sixteen year old.

'I thought you didn't want anyone to know you were back.'

'I'm sure she'll be discreet if I ask her not to spread it around.'

'Charm her will you?' Tori tripped out of the room as outside tyres crunched on the gravel. 'Good luck with that.'

***

Rhiannon circled the white Toyota like a policeman inspecting a stolen vehicle. The number plate matched the car that had stopped in Mt. Ingall's Road and the Avis sign was clearly visible through the front windscreen.

She took a deep breath, relaxed her shoulders and let go of the tension. The Reids had a visitor. It was nothing more sinister than that.

She looked towards the brick, Federation style homestead with its five chimneys and wide, wrap-around verandah and debated whether to continue with her visit or head straight into work. She wouldn't be able to discuss Jed's health problems with a visitor present. There was a good chance he'd order her off the property on sight. On the other hand, she'd made a special trip. The least she could do was suggest he make an appointment to come into town and hear out Doc. Warner's concerns.

With her course of action decided, Rhiannon ran lightly up the steps and rang the doorbell. She hadn't met Jed when she'd first visited Bindarra Downs fifteen years ago. He'd been outside working on the property the day Cameron had brought her over to meet his mother and baby sister.

A door banged somewhere inside followed by the sound of footsteps on the hardwood floor. Rhiannon held her breath and listened for Jed's shuffling gait, but the tread was too decisive, too heavy to be Tori or her father. A shadow appeared behind the stained glass panel. The door opened and Cameron Reid peered at her through the screen mesh.

Rhiannon stood stock still, too surprised to do anything more.

'Can I help you?' His voice had deepened over the years, the words delivered with a neutrality that was neither friendly nor uninviting.

'Oh, hi!' She brushed her hair away from her face. 'I'm the local nurse. I'm here to see your father.'

It couldn't be common knowledge Cameron was home on leave, that kind of news didn't escape the bush telegraph. And May had known she was heading out here this morning—she would have said something for sure.

Bluey grey eyes studied her face as he stepped onto the verandah. In fifteen years he'd grown from a lanky, good looking adolescent into a lean, mean fighting machine. Six foot four of vertical and around one hundred kilos of solid muscle, Cameron Reid sported a longer than regulation haircut and a 'let me deal with it' expression.

'Why do you want to see Jed?' he asked.

Aware of her thumping heart, Rhiannon managed to hold his direct gaze. 'There's an issue we need to discuss. He hasn't mentioned it?'

A quick shake of his head. 'I got the impression he doesn't want to see you.'

'He never wants to see me.' Rhiannon smiled a little to soften her words. Despite butting heads with Jed, she liked the man.

'I'm sorry, I don't really know what's going on. I've only just arrived.'

'I know.' She tipped her head in the direction of the Toyota. 'You stopped for me earlier, scared the living daylights out of me.'

Dark eyebrows shot up in surprise. 'That was *you?*'

'Yes. Why did you do that?'

There was an awkward pause and then his gaze left her face to slide down her body to the leather lace-ups she always wore for work. 'It was the flash from your shoes. Where I've come from, that never means anything good.'

A chill slipped down Rhiannon's spine. She knew Cameron had been in the Middle East as part of a Special Forces unit. What did he mean? A flash of gunfire, an IED?

'I'm sorry if I alarmed you,' he was saying.

'That's okay. Sounds like you acted on instinct.'

When he didn't say anymore she turned away. 'Anyway, say hello to Jed for me. Tell him I'll call by another time, I'm sure he'll be thrilled.'

'Hang on a minute.'

Rhiannon halted at the top of the stairs.

'You look familiar, do we know each other?'

With her heart pounding against her ribs, she turned to face one of the nicest boys she'd met during her adolescent years. 'Nice' was an inadequate description of him now. The man who stood before her was virile and dangerously sexy.

His gaze dipped to her left breast. 'Nurse Scott.'

He was scrutinizing her name badge so why did she feel like he was also scrutinizing a part of her anatomy?

'We met many years ago.' The words came out in a rush and she waved a hand in the direction of the property which backed onto Bindarra Downs. 'There was a junior tennis tournament. I was billeted at the Jacobs's for two weeks. You brought me over here to go horse riding.'

A spark of comprehension flashed in his eyes. 'I remember.'

'I didn't expect you to, it was a long time ago.'

'I never forget a pretty face ... Rhiannon, and you haven't changed that much.'

He remembered her name!

Heat warmed Rhiannon's cheeks and tiny sparks of pleasure tingled all the way to her toes.

Oh really? Was she blushing? Hadn't her body forgotten how to do that?

'I have less pimples,' she said with a laugh, trying not to show how easily he'd disarmed her. 'One of the benefits of reaching thirty I guess.'

'You and me both.' He smiled, a sudden flash of straight, white teeth.

For long moments he studied her face, mouth curved in a smile as if he was genuinely pleased to see her.

Then all at once he gave a quick shake of his head as though he might have been caught out daydreaming. 'Alright, I'll have a word to Dad. I can't promise anything. He can be a stubborn old bugger sometimes. I'm guessing this issue has something to do with his Parkinson's?'

'It's related, yes. And just so you're aware, I've never told your family I've been here before. I thought that would be a bit weird with you being away.'

'Okay. Whatever you feel comfortable with.'

Rhiannon smiled again. Despite the intervening fifteen years and the horrors of war, it appeared Cameron Reid still possessed the same solid core of decency he'd displayed as a teenager.

'Well, it's been nice seeing you again Cameron. I'll let you get back to your family. I'm sure you have lots of catching up to do.'

'Wait! Weren't you from Sydney? What brings you back to Bindarra Creek?'

'Maybe I'll tell you one day.' Rhiannon stepped back and raised a hand in farewell, and then, so as not to make her parting words sound too much like an invitation. 'When you have a week to spare.'

CHAPTER FOUR

'Had a busy morning Rhiannon?'

'It's been crazy.' Rhiannon peeled off her surgical gloves and dropped them in the waste disposal bin. Kevin Strickland, the high school principal, was rolling down his shirt sleeve covering the arm she'd just jabbed with a needle. 'I've weighed four babies, dressed two wounds, removed one lot of stitches and now given you your immunizations for India.'

Kevin began buttoning his shirt cuff. 'Gees, the good doctor must have been cheering the day you came to town.'

Rhiannon flushed at the compliment. She was still adjusting to the way country people expressed their gratitude for things people in the city took for granted.

'Sit in the waiting room for fifteen minutes, Kevin, if you wouldn't mind.' She began washing her hands in the small basin located in the corner of the nurse's room in

Doc. Warner's surgery. 'Some people can have an allergic reaction.'

'Righto. Today must be vaccine day.' Kevin looked around for his keys and wallet. 'Are we still good for this afternoon?'

'Sure am. See you at the school?'

'I can't wait.' Kevin said dryly, rolling his eyes. 'I just love student inoculations. I can't believe the melodrama over one little German measles jab.'

Rhiannon laughed and opened the door. 'They're teenagers. They thrive on melodrama. Better prepare the sick bay.'

'Righto.' Kevin raised a hand in farewell. 'See you later on.'

As Kevin headed for the waiting room, Rhiannon checked her watch. Half an hour until her next patient arrived. She grabbed her jacket from where it hung on the back of her chair. She'd been so busy she hadn't let May know the only threat the Toyota driver posed was to her peace of mind. She'd thought of nothing else but Cameron Reid all the way to work.

She couldn't believe the symptoms she'd first exhibited as a teenager had reoccurred at the sight of him. The racing heart, the surge of heat, the stumbling speech. It was embarrassing! She hadn't seen the man for fifteen years though from time to time he'd crossed her mind. She'd even dreamed of him on the odd occasion. One night, she'd typed his name into a social media site but the search had shown up empty. It wasn't until she'd paid a visit to the Jacobs family shortly after her arrival in Bindarra Creek that she'd learned Cameron was stationed in Iraq as part of an elite SAS unit.

And now he was home.

For how long? Two weeks? One month?

Rhiannon banished the questions from her mind. Cameron's leave duration was of no consequence to her. If she won the defamation suit, she'd be back working in Sydney in no time.

On her way out she stopped by the reception desk. 'Can I pick up anything for you while I'm out, Suellen?'

Suellen Porter arched her back, grimaced and spread her hands across her swollen belly. 'No thanks. I'm all good.'

Despite Suellen's assurances, it was obvious from the dark circles under her eyes she was tired and uncomfortable. 'Is the baby keeping you awake at night?'

The receptionist flicked her long, red ponytail over her shoulder and shifted in the swivel chair. 'On and off. My back's aching, but I don't want to take anything.'

'It's normal for the final trimester.' Rhiannon gave the eighteen year old a reassuring smile. 'I need to pop out before my next patient arrives. Would you like me to heat you up a wheat bag when I get back?'

'Oh that would be great, thanks Rhiannon.'

Rhiannon hesitated. There was a sensitive topic she needed to raise with Suellen that she'd been putting off. Doc. Warner would be losing both of them in the next four to six weeks and it was time they got something organised. 'Have you given some thought to when you'll be going on maternity leave?'

Suellen's green eyes clouded with worry. 'I want to work right up until the baby's born if I can.'

Rhiannon could understand her concern over her job. Suellen had been lucky to find work in Bindarra Creek. The town offered little in the way of employment opportunities for teenage mothers who'd dropped out of school early. Many of them relied on government support. Not Suellen. She was determined to hold onto her job now she'd found one.

'Of course you can work right up until your due date, but we have to organise a temp while you're on maternity leave. I'm going back to Sydney in six weeks. We have to get organised. We can't leave Doc. Warner in the lurch.'

A flush stained the girl's cheeks making her freckles stand out more than usual. 'Okay. I'll think about it and give you a date.'

'Thanks. That would be great.' Rhiannon opened the door, making a mental note to check Suellen's blood pressure and temperature when she got back to the surgery. She needed to ease her own mind that the flush she'd noticed was harmless.

Outside, she hurried along River Road, a crisp autumn breeze lifting her hair. She passed the hairdressing salon and women's boutique then turned right at the legal office on the corner. On Main Street, she glanced into the newsagency where she'd spotted the stranger the second time. Today, the shop was empty, save for an elderly man standing at the counter scratching his instant lottery ticket.

Rhiannon crossed the road at the cenotaph, recalling the day Mr. & Mrs. Jacobs had told her Jed's son was stationed with the SAS. After that, every time she passed the memorial she said a silent thank you no-one was laying a wreath for Cameron Reid. But there was no need for such thankyou's this morning.

Cameron was back in Bindarra Creek.

At the pub, she turned into Court Street and the memories came flooding back. On her left were the tennis courts, now underutilised, their condition barely passable. Fifteen years ago, she'd won the junior girls country championship here. Cameron had a casual job at the cinema across the road. On the second day, he'd walked over to check out the girls. After eyeing one another off, they'd struck up a conversation. He'd come to watch her play every day after that. In the early evenings, she'd meet him by the boundary fence that separated the Jacobs's property from Bindarra Downs. It was down by that fence that they'd shared their first kiss.

Rhiannon pushed aside the memories and jogged up the steps of the community hall where every Monday the Country Women's Association held their weekly craft mornings. Cameron could have a girlfriend for all she knew. Anyway, he'd be gone again soon, returning to his regiment and the danger he faced every day, while she had a different kind of battle to win.

Inside the hall, the newly installed heavy green and gold curtain was drawn across the stage, the tables and chairs arranged in a herringbone pattern. Rubber soles silent on the hardwood floor, she weaved her way through the tables searching for May among a sea of grey hair.

It wasn't long before she spotted her landlady, sitting in the middle of a beehive of women, all gifted with the skill of working and talking at the same time. On May's right sat Vera Wilson, an overly made-up woman with a silver, blunt cut bob. On her left was the thin figure of Kathleen Sullivan. Kathleen looked up as Rhiannon approached, white hair combed back and secured in a severe bun.

'Hello, Rhiannon. What do you think of the improvements to our hall?'

Rhiannon cast a critical eye around the hall. The new roof and windows courtesy of a government grant had definitely made the place warmer. 'It's a lot less draughty in here than it used to be, and I like the new green and gold stage curtain ... very Australian.'

Kathleen gave a thin smile. 'It's a long process, but we're getting there.'

'Sure.' Rhiannon looked down at the women's work spread out on the table. For months they'd been making items for the New England Regional Show which was taking place in a few weeks' time. Some were displaying their wares as part of a larger exhibition while others were entering their creations in various competitions.

'Oh, this is cute, May!' Rhiannon picked up a tiny, snow white jacket with a matching bonnet. 'I haven't seen this one.'

'She's entering that one in the show,' said Kathleen, 'along with a few of her others.'

A surge of pride bloomed in Rhiannon's chest as she fingered the soft woollen jacket no bigger than a doll's outfit. May loved making items for the pre-mature babies in Armidale's neo-natal unit, keeping them stocked with miniature pieces that couldn't be bought in the shops.

'I still have to finish the matching booties and mittens,' said May. 'I can only knit on the days when my arthritis isn't playing up.' She frowned at Rhiannon. 'What brings you down here lovey, is everything alright?'

'Everything's fine.' She glanced at May's companions. 'Can I borrow her for a minute?'

She waited as May came out from behind the table then took the other woman's arm to support her a little. 'I wanted to tell you there's no need to make enquiries about the Toyota I was telling you about. Have you mentioned it to anyone yet?'

May shook her head. 'I was going to bring it up at cuppa tea time.'

'I'm glad I caught you then. It was parked in the driveway at Bindarra Downs.' Rhiannon lowered her voice. 'Cameron Reid's home on leave.'

May's eyes widened. '*He* was the one who stopped for you?'

'Yes. Did you know he was coming home?'

May shook her head. 'Nobody mentioned it to me.'

'I wonder why he kept it hush hush?'

'I don't know. Maybe he's here for a flying visit and he wants to spend it with his Dad and Tori.'

'You could be right.' Rhiannon ignored the unexpected pang of disappointment in her chest at the thought of Cameron departing as promptly as he'd arrived. 'You were right, May. I was stressing about nothing.'

'I'm relieved too, but I'll still ask about the stranger you've noticed.'

A bell rang summoning the women to morning tea.

'Do you have time for a cuppa?' asked May.

'No, unfortunately.' Rhiannon gave May's arm a gentle squeeze. 'I'd love to stay and look at all the amazing work you ladies have done but I have to get back to the surgery.'

'Never mind, you'll see them at the show.'

'I'm looking forward to it.' Rhiannon raised her voice over a synchronised scraping of chairs as the women rose and headed into the kitchen. 'I've never been to a country show before, only the Royal Easter Show in Sydney.'

'Well, you'll get to see the largest bull in the Southern Hemisphere as well as a lot of strapping young country lads.'

Rhiannon laughed. 'In that case I wouldn't miss it.' She leaned over and kissed the older woman's delicate cheek. 'Maybe we should keep Cameron's visit to ourselves. I wouldn't like him to think I'd spread the word around, I know I caught them unawares this morning.'

May patted her back as she turned to leave. 'Whatever you say, lovey.'

***

May watched Rhiannon exit the hall, the beginnings of a plan forming in her mind.

'Have you convinced her to stay yet?' Vera Wilson drew level, a cup of tea in her hand.

'I'm working on it.'

'You'd better hurry. The town needs that girl.'

'Jog my memory, Vera. Didn't Miriam Jacobs tell you Rhiannon had become friendly with Cam Reid when she was here as a teenager?'

'Yes. Why?'

May hesitated. She didn't like breaking her word, but desperate situations called for desperate measures. 'I might have just learned something I can work with but we'd have to keep it to ourselves.'

Vera laid a hand on her chest. 'You can trust me, May. I wouldn't tell a soul.'

'Yes ... well ...' May leaned closer and spoke in a hushed tone. 'Cam's home on leave apparently. Rhiannon saw him this morning when she went out there.'

The surprise on Vera's face was all the confirmation May needed that Cam's visit wasn't common knowledge among the locals.

'How lovely for Jed and Tori!'

'And perhaps for Rhiannon as well.'

'Rhiannon?'

May sighed. Vera could be slow on the uptake sometimes.

Suddenly her companion chortled with laughter. 'Oh, you silly old fool, May. You've been reading too much 'Emma'. Don't you go playing matchmaker now.'

'Why not? Don't you remember the excitement of first love, Vera Wilson?'

'Yes, but Cam and Rhiannon were only in high school back then.'

'There's a sparkle in Rhiannon's eye I haven't seen since she moved here. And before you shout me down, I know what I'm talking about, I live with her.'

Vera took a sip of her tea. 'And the sparkle was put there by Cam?'

'What else would it be?'

'Maybe she's looking forward to going home and the horrible defamation case being over and done with.'

May didn't want to believe that. She wanted to believe it was Cam.

'For someone who attends the old time dances looking for a man, you haven't got a romantic bone in your body, Vera Wilson.'

Vera's expression turned scandalized. 'I'm not looking for a man! I go because I like dancing.'

May couldn't think of anything worse. She'd much rather knit in front of the fire or watch an ABC special on the royal family. But she loved it when love bloomed among the young people, though many needed a cattle prod to jolt them along. She feared Rhiannon was worse than most. She'd heard on the grapevine a few men had asked her out only to be knocked back with a resounding no.

'You may laugh, Vera, but I can see them together.' Cam was in a league of his own in May's opinion and she was a good judge of men. She'd chosen Mr. Bannister after all, God rest his soul. And she hadn't heard Cam was involved with anyone. How could he be when he was overseas fighting terrorists?

Vera slid her cup and saucer onto the nearest table. 'Can I get you a nice cup of tea and a scone?'

May sighed and patted her friend's arm. 'I'll come with you, Vera, and don't take any notice of my fanciful ramblings, I just want Rhiannon to be happy. That drug-taking doctor hurt her badly.'

CHAPTER FIVE

'*That* was a top meal.' Cameron drained his beer glass and placed it on the table next to the remnants of their lunch. 'You still cook a mean barbecue Dad.'

'Tori knows your appetite. She stocked the fridge ready for your arrival.' They'd been talking ever since Tori's ride to school had turned up, mostly about sport and Bindarra Downs.

Jed reached for another beer and Cameron half rose from his seat. 'Want me to open that?'

'Sit down,' Jed scowled. 'I'm not completely useless yet.'

Cameron settled back in his chair with a wry smile. 'Don't get so defensive, Dad. You're not like this with Tori are you?'

'Like what?'

'Snarling whenever she tries to help.'

He watched Jed crack open the bottle and though his father's hand was a little shaky he managed to pour the beer without spilling a drop.

'Your sister and I get along just fine. She worries about me too much.'

Poor Tori. Cameron's heart contracted in his chest. She'd put up with Jed's disappointment and frustration for years since the diagnosis, shouldering more and more of the burden as their father's body weakened under the relentless march of the disease.

'And what about Nurse Scott?' he asked, still amazed that Rhiannon was back in Bindarra Creek. They'd exchanged a few emails after she'd returned to Sydney, but he'd stopped corresponding when his mother died, unable to articulate his grief even in a letter.

'Nurse Scott.' Jed rolled his eyes. 'I don't have anything against her personally.'

'What does she want to talk to you about?' It might be a touchy subject but they had to get around to it at some stage.

'Pete Warner sends her out here from time to time. I've already told him I don't want the operation.'

'Shouldn't you consider it? We have the funds.'

'And risk becoming a vegetable? I couldn't do that to your sister, couldn't take the risk especially when you were away. I might not be in the best of shape but at least I'm here.'

'Maybe Doc. Warner thinks it's time you reconsidered.'

'He's not the one who has to have holes drilled in his head.'

Fair enough. Jed was a proud man, and though stubborn, far from stupid. Whether he went ahead with the radical procedure was entirely up to him.

'We've got nothing to lose by finding out as much as we can about it.' He might even get to see Rhiannon again. She'd appeared on the verandah this morning like a dream from a past life. A living, breathing, welcome home present minus a ring on her finger. And to think Tori had been complaining they weren't having any sort of celebration.

Jed raised his glass. 'You shouldn't have another beer if you're picking Tori up.'

'One's enough anyway.' Cameron pushed himself to his feet and began gathering their plates together. 'Thanks to special services, I've lost my tolerance.'

'That's not a bad thing. Nothing wrong with a couple of beers after work but there's too much drinking and drug taking going on in this town. Lot of young people with a lot of problems.'

Cameron carried the plates into the kitchen and stacked them in the dishwasher. He'd been luckier than most being brought up on a property like Bindarra Downs. While farming was hard work, at least he'd been spared having to leave his family for the city.

Still, he'd left Bindarra Creek for a different type of jungle.

The worst kind.

He glanced at the time. Just before 2.00 pm. An hour until he had to leave to pick up Tori. Perhaps he'd use the time to find out how many casual hands his father employed around the place and what they were doing. It was easy for workers to slacken off when they didn't have an able bodied owner looking over their shoulder.

'What do you usually do while Tori's at school?' he asked as Jed came into the kitchen.

'I haven't resorted to daytime TV if that's what you're getting at. Nothing worth watching on the box, only doctors giving relationship advice and panels of women giving their views on everything.'

Cameron grinned and set the dishwasher on its cycle. Jed was an irascible old bugger, his bark worse than his bite. Rhiannon would have had a hard time dealing with him.

'I suppose I should prove I'm not a complete invalid. Come with me. I've been working on something closer to home.'

Intrigued, Cameron followed his father out the side door to the vegetable garden where row upon row of built-up garden beds flourished with a variety of red and leafy green vegetables.

'You've got the vegie garden looking great, Dad.' Cameron stood and admired the healthy crop, pleased his father was keeping occupied and hadn't lost his sense of purpose.

'Not that!'

He looked around to see Jed heading along the path which led to the garage. Separated from the house by the vegetable garden, the garage was an independent brick structure with a mezzanine level and a concrete floor, large enough to house four cars and a variety of farming equipment.

Cameron hovered behind, debating whether now would be a good time to suggest they think about purchasing a walker. Since his last visit, Jed's previously long strides had shortened in length and were executed with variable timing.

Cameron took a deep breath and decided to say nothing. He needed to be in possession of all the facts, otherwise he'd just be going over old ground if Jed had been offered aids and rejected the lot.

He watched as Jed took a remote from his pocket and pointed it at the roller door. A metallic groan signalled the need for a coat of silicon spray. The Range Rover, now sporting a set of black and yellow learner plates, stood in its usual spot at the front. Beside it was the Polaris, a high performance off road quad complete with roll bar they used for herding cattle. Behind the Polaris was the ride-on mower, a necessity for cutting the lawns around the homestead. In the far corner, protected by a silver cover stood their expensive hobby, a 1952 vintage MG TD which he and Jed had purchased the first time Cameron had come home on leave.

'When the medication kicks in and my hands are steady, I've been doing some work on Lucille.'

'Really? Which part?'

'Why don't you take a look?'

Cameron walked over to the car and squatted at the front end. Reaching under the front bumper, he took hold of the elastic hem and lifted the cover over the front number plate.

Ignoring the scar tissue burning in his quadriceps, he straightened and began folding back the cover. Little by little, a fully restored, two door, gleaming red roadster emerged.

'Dad.' Cameron's vision blurred. It was a labour of love of mammoth proportions. 'You finished it.'

Jed's hand came down on his shoulder, his voice gruff. 'I'm not one to get on my knees and pray, mate. This was my way of feeling close to you.'

Cameron turned and embraced his father, too overcome to utter the words he longed to say. He wanted to say sorry. Sorry that his mother had died, sorry he'd left three years later while Jed was still grieving and caring for a four year old. Sorry that his father had lost his health.

'Sorry it took me so long to get discharged,' he managed to get out. 'I would have been home earlier...'

'The army don't let good men like you go easily. It was sensible to wait for the honourable discharge. The injury to your leg,' Jed loosened his hold and held up one hand, 'and this complaint, we have to look on them as a blessing in disguise.'

'I'll never look at Parkinson's as a blessing.' Cameron hated the disease, hated what it was doing to his father.

'There are worse things, mate. I might be confined close to the house but I got this little beauty finished. Silver linings and all that crap.'

Cameron blinked away the mist in his eyes and smiled. It would be a while before he composed himself enough to run his hands over the shining red panels, the black running boards and the saddle brown leather interior of the TD.

'*Jesus*, Dad, I thought you were talking about the vegetable garden. I can't believe it. *Thank you.*'

'It's your welcome home present ... for coming back safe. That's all that matters.'

Cameron turned into the high school car park and swung the Range Rover into an empty parking space. It would have been easier to bring the rental, but according to Jed, Tori hadn't had a drive in a while and would insist on driving home.

He killed the engine and with a tired groan let his head fall back against the headrest. A lack of sleep coupled with an emotional homecoming had left him with a cracker of a headache. He took a few deep breaths and tried to relax. Hopefully he'd be able to swing a couple of hour's shut-eye this afternoon.

Cameron jumped as a door slammed and an engine started. He blinked hard and tried clearing his head. The car park was emptying rapidly as teenagers in regulation school uniform filed out of the assembly hall. According to the clock on the dash, he'd been asleep for ten minutes.

Fifteen minutes later he was beginning to fear his sister hadn't received his text message when Tori came around the corner, backpack hoisted over one shoulder, deep in conversation with another girl.

As the pair drew closer it became clear Tori's companion wasn't another student but a woman, the very woman he'd been thinking about on and off since their meeting this morning. Slightly taller than his sister, Rhiannon's shining brown hair fell around her shoulders in soft waves. Suddenly, Cameron wanted to look into those chocolate brown eyes and see if she stared back at him with the same intensity as she had this morning.

Before he knew it he was out of the car and walking across the car park to greet them.

'Hi Cam, sorry I'm late.' Tori gave him an apologetic smile. 'I was talking to Rhiannon about my subject choices.'

'That's alright.' He smiled at Rhiannon. 'Hello again.'

'Can I drive?' interrupted Tori.

'Sure. Go put the L Plates on. They're in the glove box.'

He watched Tori dash away with the same purpose she'd displayed since she'd first learned to walk, doing countless laps of the verandah each day. 'I didn't expect to see you again so soon, especially in the school yard.'

He turned to find Rhiannon studying him with interest, a warmth in her eyes and a smile on her lips that transported him to another time. A simpler time, when he was young and brash and had no hesitation about leaning over and kissing her in response to that look.

Heat, stronger than the sun, warmed Cameron's body. He should ask Tori more about Rhiannon. What if she were still single? What if she still felt the attraction he way he did?

What if it was all wishful thinking on his part?

'I've been giving the students their inoculations.' She raised a hand to shade her eyes from the sun. 'Kevin and I arranged to do it last period so he didn't end up with a whole bunch of kids in the sick bay trying to skip class.'

'Oh,' he said, wondering who Kevin was.

'Kevin is the school principal. Kevin Strickland.'

'Oh, right. Well, I'm pleased I ran into you. Can I have a word?'

'Sure, go ahead.' She lowered her hand and looked around the almost deserted car park, like she was checking to see if anyone was watching. Curious, Cameron followed her gaze. Only three cars remained. The Range Rover, the blue Ford Focus which she'd driven out to Bindarra Downs that morning and a dark grey Honda.

'I spoke to Dad after you left,' he said, wondering what it was about the Honda that was holding her attention. 'He's not keen on having the operation. I get where he's coming from but I think we should find out as much as we can about it.'

'The Parkinson's operation?' Rhiannon looked up at him, squinting a little. 'Is that what Jed told you?'

'Yes. Isn't that what you came to talk to him about?'

An amused smiled played around the corners of her mouth. 'He's a cagey one, your Dad. No, that wasn't the purpose of my visit.'

Cameron blew out a frustrated breath and shifted the weight off his bad leg. 'Well, could you be more specific? I feel like I'm being given the run around.'

Her smile faded. 'You know there are privacy laws. I can't discuss Jed's health with you without him being present.'

Exasperated, Cameron swung away and headed for the car. 'Thanks for all your help.'

'Cameron! Wait! '

Like his mother, Rhiannon had always called him by his full name when everyone else in his life, apart from army personnel, called him Cam.

He halted. Ahead of him, he could see Tori through the windscreen of the Range Rover. She was sitting in the driver's seat, hands on the steering wheel, watching the exchange with interest.

He turned and faced Rhiannon.

Brown eyes full of apology, she transferred the medical bag from one hand to the other. 'I'm sorry I can't do more to help you.'

Suddenly, she looked less like the efficient nurse and more like the young girl who'd cried in his arms when her father had missed her tennis final. 'My advice would be to ask Tori why she's been missing so much school lately.'

Tori handled the car well. She'd turned out of the car park and joined the peak time traffic without a problem, if you could call Bindarra Creek's afternoon school rush peak time.

'Lucky I didn't have to merge huh?' she grinned, shooting him a quick glance. 'That's what I hate most when I drive in Armidale, merging.'

'Keep your eyes on the road.'

'Okaaay! Gees, why the sudden Grinch act?'

Cameron caught his reflection in the window. *Shit!* He really did look like the Grinch.

'What was all that about with Rhiannon?'

'Hang on a minute.' Cameron closed his eyes against the pounding headache.

'Hey! You can't close your eyes. I'm a learner driver, you're supposed to be supervising.'

'We're not under enemy fire are we?'

Though he couldn't see her, he sensed her surprise.

'Of course not ... you *idiot.*'

He smiled. 'Then everything's good. And just so you know, I feel perfectly safe. You've been driving the Polaris around the property since you were nine.'

'Finally ... some respect.'

He heard her take a deep breath and when he opened his eyes she looked happy and relaxed in the driver's seat.

He waited until they were clear of the town and on the road to Armidale before he spoke again. 'Shouldn't you be discussing your subject choices with your year advisor?'

'I want to be a nurse.'

'Really?' A warm glow began to spread throughout Cameron's body. 'You're taking after Mum?'

'Hopefully, and who better to ask than an actual nurse?'

Tori didn't remember their mother. That had been his privilege. Maybe this was Tori's way of adding to the memories, the stories and anecdotes he and Jed had tried to pass on to her.

'You'll have to improve your attendance then. I hear you've been missing school lately.'

'Rhiannon told you, didn't she?'

'Don't be mad with her, I'm sure she's got your best interests at heart.'

'So you can be mad with Rhiannon and Dad can be mad with Rhiannon, but I can't.'

Cameron puffed out his cheeks and blew out a huge breath. *Jesus!* Ordering his men around was easier than this.

'Don't worry, Cam, I'm not mad with Rhiannon for dobbing. We're good friends.'

'Really? She's a lot older than you.'

'You're a lot older than me, geriatric if this music's anything to go by.' Tori leaned over and pressed the seek button on the radio. 'What's wrong with Triple JJJ?'

'I *like* classical music.'

'Since when?'

Since screaming rock stars began to sound like the screams of dying men.

'I prefer music without the singing. It's relaxing.'

Tori turned the radio off. 'The station Dad listens to is better than this.'

Cameron smiled. It really was good to be home. 'How do you know Rhiannon?'

Tori shrugged. 'Just from Doc. Warner's surgery.'

Thirty five years ago his mother had worked for Doc. Warner. No wonder Jed had a hard time dealing with Rhiannon. She had to bring back memories of his mother in some way.

'She's given me a lot of useful information on the challenges of being a carer.'

A carer.

Tori's total acceptance of what she'd had to become for their father while he'd been deployed compounded the guilty ache in Cameron's chest. He stared at the twists and turns in the road ahead, wishing he could handle these new emotions as easily as Tori handled the car.

'You've done your bit midget, now it's my turn.' He'd gone into the army at eighteen, unable to deal with the changes his father had made around the farm after his mother's death. Once enlisted, he'd learned pretty quickly people cope with death in different ways. He'd stopped judging his father then.

'So why have you been missing school?'

Despite his earlier reprimand, she glanced at him again. 'The medication works better some days more than others. Dad can have periods where there's hardly any tremor.'

'And that's when he's been able to work on Lucille?' Like Jed, he was looking for silver linings.

'You've seen her, haven't you?' Tori's face broke into a delighted smile. 'Isn't she beautiful?'

'She sure is.'

They were quiet for a few moments, each lost in their own thoughts.

'So tell me about the bad days.' The trip home took fifteen minutes door to door. At this point, he was going to need every minute of it.

'Sometimes, he's so stiff in the mornings he has to crawl out of bed before he can walk.'

Cameron rested an elbow on the sill and rubbed his temple with his thumb. He was beginning to understand. Jed was a proud man. He'd hate anyone seeing him like that, especially his daughter. 'And of course you couldn't leave him at home alone could you?'

Tori shook her head, bottom lip quivering, eyes trained straight ahead.

Cameron's stomach muscles clenched while he held his breath. He wanted to tell her to pull over but he forced himself to stay quiet. Tori wasn't a child anymore.

'A couple of times he really scared me.'

He blew out a breath and dragged in another. 'What do you mean? Is that why Rhiannon wants to talk to him?'

Tori nodded. 'I've been driving the car to school in the mornings. Usually, the medication's working by the time he has to drive home. But lately, it hasn't been kicking in fast enough. The first time it happened, I wanted to turn around and drive him back home but he made me get out and go into school. I was worried sick. Eventually I asked principal Strickland if I could call home and check. Dad can't use a phone when he's shaking badly.'

'How many times has this happened?'

'Six or seven. Eventually, Mr. Strickland told Doc. Warner and that's when Rhiannon got involved. I haven't missed that much class time. Sometimes I get a lift with Mr. McGregor if I ring early enough.'

'You should have told me about this Tori, I would have spoken to Dad. He shouldn't be driving.'

'I know ... but you haven't been here and someone in the family needed to have a license. How was I going to get the hundred hours in my logbook if Dad relinquished his? At least he can sit in the passenger seat while I drive.'

Cameron took another deep breath and steadied himself. Finally, he was getting somewhere.

'Has Pete Warner asked Dad to hand in his licence?'

Tori nodded. 'Dad told him where to go. Lucky they're friends. Now Rhiannon's checking on him during the day.'

And trying to talk some sense into him by the sound of it. Rhiannon was right. His father was a cagey old bugger. But risking his life was completely unacceptable. By the sound of it, Pete Warner, Rhiannon and even this Principal Strickland had been trying their best to help the family in what was clearly a difficult situation.

Cameron clenched his jaw and held onto his disappointment. Bindarra Creek was a town that rallied together to help families in need, but it seemed Jed was too proud to accept what he saw as charity.

Or pity.

And that was a failing of his father.

CHAPTER SIX

Doc. Warner angled his face so the reflected light rays from his head mirror shone squarely onto the patient's injured finger. 'Nothing like finishing the day with a bit of micro surgery, Mrs. Tate.'

Mrs. Tate had arrived with her hand wrapped in a bloodied towel. She'd been washing dishes, scouring the inside of a coffee mug when the mug had slipped and hit the bottom of the sink. Unbeknownst to her, the mug had cracked and broken apart. As she'd continued with the twisting motion, the sharp edge of the broken mug had sliced through the knuckle of her right middle finger.

Mrs. Tate bit down on her bottom lip and averted her face as Doc. Warner began sewing together the jagged pieces of lacerated skin. Six stitches later, he knotted the thread and held up the ends.

'Just there, thank you.'

Rhiannon leaned over and cut the thread.

Mrs. Tate gave the elderly doctor a grateful smile. 'Thank you, Doctor. I was lucky I got here before you closed.'

'We seem to be staying later and later every day, isn't that right, Rhiannon?'

Rhiannon nodded and smiled, watching as he put an arm behind the woman's back and helped bring her up into a sitting position. 'Are you feeling alright now, Mrs. Tate?'

'I'm a little woozy, but I'll be fine.'

Doc. Warner nodded. 'I'll leave you in Rhiannon's capable hands. She'll dress the wound for you. Take care now.'

'Bye, bye, doctor.'

Doc. Warner left the room, limping slightly. He'd already had one knee replacement and was overdue for another.

Rhiannon took surgical dressing and tape down from the cupboard. 'Try and keep this dry, if you can. You'll have to cover it with a plastic bag when you shower. Secure it at the wrist with a strong rubber band.' She opened the paper packet and began applying the dressing to the woman's finger. 'It's a pretty drastic way of getting out of the washing up.'

The woman laughed, the colour returning to her face. 'It happened so quickly, and it bled so much. I had to get my daughter to drive me here.'

'It's a nasty one. I could see into the joint cavity.' She'd definitely brushed up on her general nursing skills since moving to Bindarra Creek, the town not being large enough to warrant a dedicated midwife.

The woman looked down at her bandaged finger. 'Are they the type of stitches that dissolve?'

'No, they'll have to be taken out. Make an appointment with Suellen for about ten days' time.'

That's right, she needed to speak with Doc. Warner about Suellen's maternity leave.

A short while later Rhiannon knocked softly on the doctor's open door. 'Excuse me, Peter.'

'Come in.' Doc. Warner removed the head mirror and laid it on the desk.

'I asked Suellen when she'd like to finish up. She's going to give me a date.'

'That's good to hear. Thank you, Rhiannon.' He unhooked his jacket from the coat rack in the corner. 'I spoke to my sister-in-law. She's fine to come back and fill in. She just needs the dates so they don't plan a holiday during that time.'

Rhiannon breathed a sigh of relief. 'Suellen will be pleased. I get the feeling she's insecure—scared almost that if she takes time off she'll lose her job.'

'Why? I'm pleased with how she's going. My sister-in-law's not interested in returning to work. She and my brother are pretty much retired.'

'Maybe Suellen needs to hear that from you,' Rhiannon suggested tentatively.

Doc. Warner shrugged on his brown checked sports jacket, the one he always wore to and from work. 'I'll make sure she knows. How'd you'd go this morning, with Jed?'

'No luck. I turned up at a bad time. His son had just arrived home.'

'Cam?' Doc. Warner shot her a surprised look. 'I didn't know he was home.'

'I don't think anyone did.'

'I'll have to have a beer with him.'

They switched off the lights, set the alarm and exited the surgery together. 'You seem very fond of Cameron,' Rhiannon said, hoping she didn't sound too nosey.

'He's my godson!'

'*Really?*' It was Rhiannon's turn to be surprised. Doc. Warner was closer to Cameron's family than she'd realised. No wonder he'd found raising the licence problem with Jed so difficult.

'My wife will be pleased ... she has a real soft spot for Cam.'

She isn't the only one!

Flustered by the thought that popped into her head, Rhiannon pointed her key fob at her Ford Focus, watching as Doc. Warner put his medical bag in the boot. He walked along to the driver's door, his limp reminding her of the way Cameron had walked towards her at the school today. She hadn't noticed it this morning when he'd stepped out onto the verandah. Now she'd finished work, her mind filled with questions.

What was the nature of his injury?

Was he home on medical leave?

For how long?

She bade Doc. Warner goodnight, climbed into her vehicle and switched on her headlights. She had to stop thinking about Cameron. She *did* have a soft spot for him, and for Tori, but it was vital she retain a professional distance from the complicated family situation he was dealing with now he was home. It would be all too easy to become emotionally involved, and no good could come of that. She was leaving in six weeks. It was going to be hard enough saying goodbye to the people of Bindarra Creek as it was.

Rhiannon pulled out of the car park and headed for the service station on the other side of the river. Despite the approach of spring, the evenings remained bitterly cold. The shops were in darkness, the streetlights shining on an almost deserted roadway. Apart from one man walking his dog, it appeared the locals had retreated inside for the night.

Five minutes later, she pulled into a service station, filled the tank and picked up a carton of milk for May. She was lining up at the counter when a gunmetal grey Honda pulled into the bowser behind her car. A thickset, fair haired man with a buzz cut climbed from the car and scanned the windows of the service centre as though looking for someone.

Rhiannon's scalp crawled, the hairs on her forearms standing on end. It was the stranger she'd seen around town, the man May was making enquiries about. And she'd noticed the Honda before. It had been parked outside the newsagency the day she'd spotted the man inside, and again in the school car park while she'd been talking to Cameron.

Heart pounding, Rhiannon edged forward in the line. Eyes trained on the stranger, she groped in her handbag for her wallet.

As she watched, he picked up a bucket and window brush, leaned across the bonnet and started cleaning his windscreen.

No petrol.

No reason to come into the service centre and pay.

'Swipe your card, please.'

Rhiannon tore her gaze away from the man and did as the attendant asked. Hands trembling, she punched in her pin and waited for the transaction to process.

On the way out, she paused in front of the magazine rack, dropped her wallet back in her handbag and took out her phone. By the time she reached the bowsers, the man had abandoned his window cleaning and had put aside the bucket.

He watched her come closer, staring, squinty eyes beneath a prominent forehead.

Rhiannon opened the passenger door and threw her handbag and container of milk on the seat. Slamming the door closed, she rounded the bonnet, phone in her left hand, keys in her right. Before the man could climb into his car, she lifted her phone, steadied her trembling hand and took a photograph.

Rhiannon wrenched the driver's door open and slid in behind the wheel. She hit the central locking, tossed the phone onto the passenger seat and shoved the key in the ignition. Eyes on the rear view mirror, she fired up the engine and threw the car into gear. She pulled away from the bowsers a little too quickly, the Honda roaring to life behind her.

She turned into Main Street and headed back towards town. Ahead, looming in the darkness, the single lane timber truss Kingfisher Bridge straddled the banks of the Akuna River.

Rhiannon concentrated on the tail-lights of the car in front, sending up a silent plea that the traffic wasn't stopped at the bridge. In her rear view mirror, the Honda's headlights were glowing brighter as the driver closed the gap between them.

Rhiannon's stomach twisted like wild lantana. Ahead of her, three cars had come to a halt having yielded to traffic approaching the bridge from the opposite direction.

She clenched her jaw, thought about doing a three point turn and heading back to the service station, but oncoming traffic was already on the bridge. And if she turned the car around, there was only the Wildlife Rescue Centre along the isolated road to Moree.

Rhiannon edged closer to the vehicle in front and let the car idle. She sank lower in the seat and watched the Honda in her rear view mirror. She had his number plate, she had his photograph and the police station was only a few blocks away on the other side of the bridge.

But what evidence did she have that this man was watching her or trying to intimidate her?

Zero.

She had nothing, only her intuition.

Could she trust it?

She'd freaked out about the white Toyota this morning and the driver had turned out to be Cameron. The man with the buzz cut, now a shadowy silhouette in the stationary car behind had done nothing but look at her.

Yet something told her he meant trouble.

White light blinded her.

She gasped, heart jumping, pulse pounding in her throat as she pressed herself into the seat and raised a forearm to her eyes. Keeping her foot planted on the brake, Rhiannon twisted in her seat. The Honda's high beam illuminated the cabin like a spotlight.

Closing her eyes against the glare, she groped for the tennis racquet she knew was in the rear footwell. Her fingertips brushed the roughened grip and she curled her fingers around the handle and dragged the racquet into her lap.

Exposed like an escapee in a helicopter searchlight, she squinted against the glare reflecting in her rear view mirror. Ears straining, foot still on the brake, she listened for the sound of a car door or the crunch of approaching footsteps on the gravel shoulder of the road.

But there was no sound apart from the idling engine and the wind stirring the ghost gums on either side of the road.

Seconds ticked by.

Breathing hard, sweat breaking out on the back of her neck, Rhiannon kept her head down and gripped the racquet.

A horn blasted and she jumped, pain shooting up her arm as she banged her elbow on the door. An oncoming road train roared past in a rush of wind, driver leaning on the horn in a loud demand for the Honda to turn down its high beam.

The cabin dimmed.

Rhiannon blinked, scalp tingling, every nerve ending in her body prickling. Three cars followed the truck, a sedan and two four wheel drives.

One by one the cars in front began to move off. Leaving the racquet in her lap, Rhiannon checked her rear view mirror again. The man was a faint outline behind the wheel.

Finally, it was her turn. She gripped the steering wheel and pressed her foot down on the accelerator. Determined not to look at the Honda until she'd safely crossed the bridge, she kept pace with the car in front, wooden planks rattling beneath the wheels in a rhythmical beat.

On the other side of the river, she passed the boarded up Riverside Pub, indicated left and got the green light. With another glance in the mirror she proceeded through the intersection, the Honda still on her tail. At the surgery she made a right-hand turn into Willow Tree Drive. With luck, the guy with the buzz cut would think she was returning to work and keep going.

He turned right and followed her.

Determined not to lead him back to May's place, Rhiannon headed for the police station, anger building inside her. She drove past Fig Tree Lodge, the bed and breakfast that backed onto the rear of the surgery then proceeded across the Mt. Ingall's Road intersection. One block further along, she crossed Court Street, and there, opposite the library stood the blue and white checkerboard sign of the police station. Lights shone from the interior of the one storey building, a highway patrol vehicle parked out front.

Rhiannon dragged in a deep breath and pulled into the curb opposite the station. Behind her, the Honda visibly slowed.

'Come on.' She put her hand on the horn, ready to sound the alert should the creep make a move. 'Show me what you're made of now.'

The car came slowly.

Rhiannon tensed, hoping he'd do a U turn and roar away, but he stopped the car in the middle of the road, nose in line with her rear bumper.

Rhiannon's breath quickened, hand poised on the horn ready to bring the police running. What was he doing? Waiting for her to get out and walk across the road? Waiting to mow her down?

Reaching into the passenger seat, she picked up her mobile phone and put it to her ear. Gaze riveted on the Honda, she reached up and flicked on the interior light. Hopefully, the man with the buzz cut would think she was phoning the officer on duty inside the station.

He fell for it. The engine revved and with a spin of tyres the Honda roared off down Willow Tree Drive.

Rhiannon closed her eyes and sagged in the seat. When she opened them, the red glow of tail lights were fading in the distance. She put her mobile in the centre console, the tennis racquet still in her lap. She wanted to go inside and report the driver. She wanted to show the officer on duty the photograph and ask if the man was known to him.

Rhiannon covered her face with her hands. She couldn't do it, not with the defamation charge against Dominic Mullen coming up for hearing, and the unfair dismissal case she'd taken against the hospital.

She'd been painted as a liar and a person who stirred up trouble, not that her friends in Bindarra Creek believed a word of it. Instead, May, Doc. Warner and others had wrapped themselves around her and supported her, refusing to believe their hard-working community nurse was capable of the things she'd been accused of.

Rhiannon lowered her hands and looked longingly at the police station, her lawyer's voice in her head.

Stay under the radar. Be discreet. Don't indulge in any behaviour that could show you in a poor light or could potentially be used against you.

If she walked into the police station waving around a photograph of Mr. Buzz Cut and accusing him of following her, there was every chance her friends in Bindarra Creek could begin to doubt the truth of her story. Not May. May knew the entire story. But others who didn't could be forgiven for thinking she was displaying the same pattern of behaviour that had brought her to Bindarra Creek in the first place. Stirring up trouble by making accusations, this time in a different town.

Rhiannon put her hands on the wheel.

She couldn't do it.

She had the man's photograph.

For now, it had to be enough.

CHAPTER SEVEN

Cameron shrugged off his shirt and threw it into the Polaris. After the suffocating heat of the Middle East, thirty-four degrees Celsius should have been a walk in the park but his injury had left him seriously out of shape.

Rivulets of sweat snaked a path between his shoulder blades as he reached into the vehicle and grabbed the water bottle. He carried it over to the fence he'd finished repairing, unscrewed the top and took a long, welcome drink.

'Beat me to it.'

He looked up to see Angus McGregor astride his black stallion, Pharaoh. The huge camphor laurel on Angus's side of the boundary fence had concealed his neighbour's approach.

Cameron smiled, watching as Angus dismounted. 'I'd forgotten how much damage dry rot can do to fence posts, Angus.'

'The mahogany's stood up better than the ironbark.' Angus reached across the barb wire to grasp Cameron's outstretched hand. 'Welcome back, Cam.'

'Thanks, mate.'

'Home for long this time?'

'For good. I appreciate you helping out the family while I've been away.'

'Just being neighbourly. You'd do the same.'

Angus was right. It was the way things worked in the country. Well, at least the way things worked in Bindarra Creek.

Angus pushed back the brim of his Akubra . 'I was on my way to check on the herd.'

'Already done.' Cameron looked towards the western boundary where a lack of rainfall had turned gentle undulating hills from green to brown. 'The bottom pastures are looking better than I expected.'

Angus had separated the steers from the cows, and over the next few days Cameron wanted to divide the herd again. Those in good condition could be sold, the heifers rearing calves brought closer to the homestead. That way, he could spell more paddocks.

They spent the next half hour discussing the long term weather forecasts, irrigation issues, river depth and the price of beef.

'Are you planning on sticking with the Herefords?' asked Angus. 'Many of the city boys are going with my namesake.'

Cameron smiled.

Angus cattle. A popular breed ... at the moment.

The Reids were three generation graziers, their farming methods traditional, their practices handed down from father to son. But it was indisputable the Hereford heifers threw a big calf with a high percentage of cows lost during birth. Many graziers had begun to cross-breed to get a smaller calf, mostly Angus cattle crossed with Murray Grey or Brahman.

'I'll stick with the Herefords, for now,' said Cameron. 'I'll be interested to see how things turn out. You?'

'I think it's worth considering.'

Angus McGregor was a good operator. He'd built Craigellachie into one of the best grazing properties in Bindarra Creek.

'Let's talk then. How about you bring Ollie around one night for a barbecue. I think he was a toddler the last time I saw him.'

'We'd like that.' Angus scooped up the reins from where he'd looped them over a fence post and mounted Pharaoh. 'The Jacobs' were a great help too. They're on holidays at the moment.'

'Maybe we can do it when they get back then.'

Cameron looked towards the rear boundary which separated Jacobs' land from Bindarra Downs. He used to meet Rhiannon on that rear boundary, right beside the silky oak. They'd climb up its massive trunk and out onto the lower boughs where, camouflaged by its leafy foliage, they'd talk for ages. He'd even got up the courage to kiss her a few times. They'd gone a bit further too, the day he'd taken her riding.

Cameron's body tightened, an image of a sexier, wiser Rhiannon uploading in his mind and replacing the youthful one he'd stored there for years.

'Be seeing you, Cam.'

Cameron raised a hand in farewell and watched Angus urge the stallion into a trot. It had been years since they'd had horses at Bindarra Downs, years since they'd even kept a working dog.

Short-circuiting his wistful thoughts before they could take hold, Cameron pulled his phone from his pocket and checked the time. One o'clock. He had time to call Rhiannon before he headed back to the homestead for lunch.

The early afternoon sun biting into his shoulders, he gathered up his tools and stacked them in the Polaris. He looked around for his shirt. It was lying in the dry grass. Strange, he could have sworn he'd thrown it on the seat. He shrugged it on, not bothering to do up the buttons. His thigh was tight in his jeans as though the exercise might have caused it to swell. Wincing, he settled himself in the Polaris as comfortably as he could. Then he scrolled through his contacts until he found the number Tori had given him last night.

***

Rhiannon put down her toasted cheese and tomato sandwich and stared at the incoming call on her mobile.

Unknown number.

Half inclined to reject it, she rubbed a hand across her tired eyes and gazed at the street from inside the Cyprus Café. She'd barely slept after her ordeal with the Honda driver, and she'd been careful to play down the incident to May. She didn't want to worry her friend.

Snatching up the phone, she swiped a thumb across the screen and put it to her ear. 'Hello.' She omitted her usual 'Rhiannon speaking'. She wasn't about to announce herself to the unknown caller, whoever it was.

'Is that Rhiannon?' Cameron's warm, deep voice flowed through the ear piece, soothing her bad mood like honey soothing a sore throat.

Hot tears pricked the backs of her eyes and she swallowed hard. 'Yes.'

'Oh, it didn't sound like you. It's Cameron Reid calling.'

I know!

'Hi, Cameron.' Rhiannon's mind went blank. She couldn't think of a single thing to say. Yesterday, she'd thought it best to keep her distance. Today, she wanted to connect with her old friend.

'Tori gave me your number. Have I caught you at a bad time?'

Her life was a bad time. How disappointing he'd called and not come to see her in person.

Oh for God's sake Rhiannon, stop feeling sorry for yourself and harden up!

According to May's information, Cameron had spent the last four years training Iraqi soldiers how to fight. And he'd returned home to a situation which was, though different to hers, every bit as onerous.

She straightened her back. 'Now's a good time. I'm on my lunch break.'

There was a brief silence. She imagined him standing on the verandah at Bindarra Downs, nodding quietly, the way he did when he was listening to other people speak.

'Tori told me everything, including why she's been missing so much school.'

Finally, some positive news! 'I'm so relieved you know, Cameron.'

'Is it true Doctor Warner's already asked my father to relinquish his license?'

'Yes. Jed didn't take it very well.'

'Lucky they're friends.' He hesitated for a few moments. 'Are you able to bring me up to speed on this?'

'Of course.' Rhiannon's heart gave an excited little skip at the thought of seeing him again. 'Would you like to come into the surgery ... or we could get a coffee and talk about it if you like?'

It was an opportunistic invitation, one she regretted the moment the words were out of her mouth.

There was a pause, then, 'Is it possible to tell me now? I have so much going on at the moment.'

'Of course.' Mortified heat flooded Rhiannon's face as she stared at the peppermint coloured laminated table top. How foolish of her to imagine he wanted to see her just because she was looking forward to seeing him.

All he wanted was the facts.

She cleared her throat and spoke as professionally as she could. 'By rights, any medical condition or impairment should be reported to the traffic authority. If the driver doesn't do it, concerned relatives and friends can. Doctor Warner and myself will have to submit that form if it gets to the point where we feel it has to be done, but please, don't get me wrong, this is not something either of us want to do. It would be so much easier for everyone if Jed reported the matter himself.'

There was another brief silence, then Cameron said. 'I understand that.'

'Will you speak to him? He's aware people are concerned.'

'Of course I'll speak to him, but I'll have to pick my time. If I give you my personal guarantee that he won't get behind the wheel of a car, can you hold off on that form?'

'I'll speak to Doctor Warner and Kevin. I'm sure they won't have a problem with that.'

'And you?'

'The same goes for me,' Rhiannon said quickly. 'That's why I've been coming out to the property, to try and convince him to hand it in voluntarily.'

'It won't be necessary for you to do that anymore. I'll be doing all the driving, including taking Tori to and from school.'

'Alright.' If she'd doubted the first rebuff, the second one told her Cameron wasn't interested in catching up with her for old time's sake or for anything else.

Swallowing her disappointment, she pushed away her plate. She hadn't been hungry to begin with, now she couldn't take another bite. 'I'll let Doctor Warner know I've left things in your hands. We'll wait to hear from you.'

'Hopefully it will be sooner rather than later.'

Another brief silence, then. 'Thanks for taking the time, Rhiannon. I appreciate it.'

'No problem. Bye Cameron.'

***

Cameron dropped the remains of his sandwich onto his plate and replayed his words in his head. *Is it possible to tell me now, I have so much going on at the moment.*

What the hell had he been thinking?

He'd been trying to take charge. Taking charge was what he did best. But he'd added insult to injury when he told her she didn't have to come out to the property anymore. It was obvious from the quiet retreat in her voice she'd taken him the wrong way.

He groaned out loud.

He was an idiot!

He didn't want Rhiannon to think he was indifferent to her. He'd liked her fifteen years ago and he still liked her. Three short conversations in a day and a half was all it had taken. He was interested. Enough to want to find out more.

Cameron put his plate in the sink and looked out the kitchen window towards the garage where Jed was tinkering with Lucille's oil pump. Should he go and speak to his father now? It was better they engage in some activity when there was serious talking to be done. The sooner he had the conversation with Jed, the sooner his father would be off the road. He'd also have something to take back to Rhiannon. Maybe he should suggest they discuss it over coffee this time. Or dinner.

A sting way down in his lower back stopped him at the door. Frowning, he rubbed a hand over his lumbar area. The sting changed to an itch then worsened, fingers of heat spreading downwards over his butt cheek.

Cameron winced.

Christ! What the hell had he done, irritated a nerve? He'd been careful of his back and leg while straightening those fence posts and re-tensioning the wire.

He slipped a hand down the back of his jeans. Right away his fingers found a hard lump, then swelling, heat and irritation.

'Ah, *shit!*

He left the kitchen and strode towards the garage. So much for his plans to talk to Jed about his licence.

He found his father pulling the cover over the TD.

'Hey, Dad.'

'I'm coming inside. I'm shaking like a leaf.'

'Can you take a look at this?' Cameron walked over to his father and unzipped his jeans. 'Tell me if it's what I think it is.'

'Will it put me off my lunch?'

'Very funny.' Cameron pushed his jeans down and bared his butt to his father. 'Down there. It feels like a tick.'

He waited while Jed leaned over and inspected his lower torso.

'Sure is. It's a paralysis tick. It's sucking the blood out of your arse.'

'Jesus!' It must have crawled onto his shirt when it was lying in the long grass.

'It's a big un.' Jed snorted with laughter. 'Burrowed in right at the top of your butt crack.'

'Okay, okay, I'm getting the picture. Do you think you can get it out with the pointy tweezers?'

'I'm not steady enough. Maybe with the pliers.'

'You're not coming anywhere near my arse with pliers.'

'You'll have to get Tori to get it out then.'

'No way! I'm not asking my *sister* to pull a tick out of my arse.' Cameron zipped up his jeans and looked at his father. 'Anyway, she has drama after school today. I don't have to pick her up until five.'

Jed looked at his watch. 'That's another four hours. You might be feeling a bit off by then. Go into town and see Pete Warner.'

Was his father overreacting? A tick could kill a dog or cat in hours but it would take a couple of days for the poison to make a guy his size seriously ill. On the other hand, the jury was out on whether Australian ticks carried Lyme disease. Why take the chance when the surrounding area was already swollen, itchy and sore? He could wait until Tori came home but he didn't like the thought of the tick feeding on him for the next four hours, especially down in that area.

'I might give Angus a call.'

Back in the house, Cameron looked up Angus's number in Jed's old-fashioned A-Z address book. Two minutes later he hung up.

'That was his housekeeper. He's gone into Armidale. I was only talking to him an hour ago. I missed him by fifteen minutes.'

'In the old days we just pulled 'em out, tore the body clear off the head. It can take a couple of days for the head to fall out.'

'That's what I'm worried about. I had a couple of allergic reactions to ticks when I was a kid, remember?'

Jed grunted.

Cameron doubted his father did remember. As a former nurse, the children's health had always been his mother's domain.

Cameron snatched up his keys, sunglasses and wallet from the hallstand. Of all the places the little blighter could bury itself, it had to choose somewhere he couldn't see. And Jed was too shaky to even hold a mirror.

'I'll have to go into the surgery, Dad.'

'I think that's your best bet. Say g'day to Pete for me.'

CHAPTER EIGHT

Cameron looked up from the dog-eared magazine he'd been reading and stared at the bubbling fish tank in Doc. Warner's waiting room. Half an hour had passed since he'd arrived and still the doctor's door remained steadfastly closed. The crowd in the waiting room were beginning to grow restless.

A three year old who'd been playing in the children's corner, picked up a bucket of coloured blocks and upended the entire contents onto the floor. Plastic blocks went flying in all directions, sliding underneath the magazine table and bouncing under the waiting room chairs.

'Oh, Jake!' bemoaned the child's mother. She sank to her knees and began gathering up the pieces. 'Come on, pick them up and put them back in the bucket.'

Cameron tucked the magazine under his arm and began helping the harassed looking mum pick up the red and yellow blocks.

'Oh, thank you,' the woman said with a grateful smile.

Cameron gritted his teeth and tried ignoring the infernal itch at the base of his spine. 'No problem.'

'Mr. Reid. Would you like to come through?'

He looked up to see Rhiannon standing in the doorway. She wore her standard nurse's uniform and a quiet smile. Yesterday she'd worn her hair down. Today, it was twisted into some kind of loose bun. Curly strands of hair framed her pretty face.

Cameron scrambled to his feet.

'Dr. Warner's running behind time.' She spoke in a quiet voice so the other patients couldn't hear. 'He's asked me to attend to your procedure.'

Cameron's stomach lurched. *Way to go Pete!*

'I don't mind waiting,' he mumbled, taking the magazine out from under his arm. He hadn't foreseen this. Sure, he'd been thinking about what to say if he bumped into her and they had a chance to talk. Something about him not meaning to sound abrupt on the phone and suggesting they do catch up for that coffee.

He hadn't bargained on dropping his pants for her.

Not yet, anyway.

'It's up to you.' Her brown eyes twinkled and she raised an eyebrow as if daring him. 'You could be in for a long wait though. There are four people ahead of you.'

You're an SAS officer for Christ sake Reid, not a wuss!

'Okay, that's fine.'

Liar!

Her gaze dipped to the magazine in his hands. 'I think that magazine's about fifteen year's old.'

Suddenly nervous, he dropped it on the table and followed her out of the room. 'Clearly animal stories don't date.'

***

She couldn't believe it!

She'd been thinking about Cameron since the phone call and now he was here in her room, all broad shoulders and long legs.

'Take a seat.' Rhiannon slid his file onto the bench. She'd read the note from Suellen. 'You have a paralysis tick somewhere you can't reach? Is it in your hair?'

They usually got in people's hair, burrowing in behind their ears or on the top of their scalp. She glanced at Cameron's thick brown hair, heart skipping a beat at the prospect of running her fingers through the silky stands.

'No.' He blushed the colour of a good Merlot and spread his hand over the lumbar region of his spine. 'It's right down there. I can't see it and Jed's too shaky to get it out.'

She couldn't remember the last time she'd seen a grown man blush. In Sydney, it just didn't happen. It was sweet.

Be professional Rhiannon!

Palms sweaty, she took a clean towel from the cupboard and placed it on the end of the examination table. 'Okay, just take off your-'

'Ah, gees.' He raked a hand through his hair and looked at her with uncertain eyes. 'I've been mending fences all morning, Rhiannon. I haven't even had a shower.'

'That's perfectly okay.'

She was a health professional.

It was up to her to put him at ease.

She turned her back and walked over to the basin. 'Drop your strides, Cameron, and lay on your stomach. The shirt can stay on, just lift it up out of the way. You can put the towel over your legs for privacy.'

When he didn't object further, she turned on the tap—hard. Over the sound of running water, she listened for audible cues, shoes coming off, a zipper lowering, the rustle of clothing as he stepped out of his jeans. She was soaping her hands when the examination table creaked beneath his weight.

She turned off the tap and tore some paper towelling from the dispenser on the wall. When she turned, he was lying on the table, arms raised above his head, towel pulled up to cover his bottom and thighs.

Rhiannon swallowed. He'd hiked up his shirt as she'd instructed revealing a mouth-watering expanse of firm, tapering, torso.

Medical terminology only!

She walked towards the table snapping on a pair of latex gloves. 'Comfortable?'

'You could say,' he said, as if through gritted teeth.

She laid a hand on the edge of the towel that covered his lumbar, a non-verbal cue she was ready to begin. 'Right. Let's take a look.'

She folded back the towel until tanned skin changed to lily white. A little further down, a reddened, irritated area the size of her palm appeared at the top of his very firm, nicely rounded buttocks.

'Yes, I see it.' She was talking about the tick but even to her it sounded like she was talking about something else.

Pushing that thought aside, she closed the pointy tweezers around the tick's gross, grey body and carefully inspected how far it was in. 'The head's completely burrowed into your intergluteal cleft. It's very engorged. Have you sprayed insect repellent on it?'

'No, should I have?'

She reached for the antiseptic, tipped some onto a cotton pad and dabbed it on the tick and surrounding area.

'It's not necessary but say for instance you're in the outback', she babbled on, trying not to notice how his skin turned to gooseflesh and his back muscles tensed. 'Insect spray will kill the tick and it will die and eventually drop off. It's always preferable to have it extracted properly, especially if you have some kind of allergic reaction, which you seem to have had.'

'Well, I'm not in the bloody outback, Rhiannon, so can you just get it out before it poisons me and something else drops off?'

Rhiannon dropped the tweezers.

At the clang, Cameron turned and looked at her, exasperation fading in his eyes. 'I'm sorry, I shouldn't have said that.'

'It's okay, I'm talking too much.' She retrieved the tweezers and put them on the bench. So much for acting professional, she'd do better if she just acted herself. 'It's you, Cameron, you're making me nervous.'

'*You're* nervous? I'm the one with my bare rump in the air!'

Though his words were indignant, his smile reached all the way to his eyes and Rhiannon couldn't help but smile back. The ice was broken, and it was like they'd stepped back in time fifteen years where they kidded around and flirted with each other.

'You *are* the one with your rump in the air, so *behave!* She fetched a second pair of sterilised tweezers from the cupboard. 'I would have thought, being a soldier, you would know the insect spray trick.'

'I've spent all my time in the Middle East. It's too dry and sandy for ticks.'

'Okay, hold still.' Aiming the tweezers, she took hold of the grey, seed shaped tick body.

'A bit of a sting now.'

Rhiannon extracted the tick with a twist and a pull. It came away, burrowing legs tearing through Cameron's skin on the way out. She dropped it into a beaker along with the tweezers and pressed a sterile gauze patch against the bleeding wound.

'There, the little vampire's out. I can't believe how much blood it sucked out of you.'

He chuckled, the same warm, rich sound she remembered, only an octave deeper. He smelled like the outdoors, all sunshine and grass mixed with denim and leather. Even through the latex gloves, his skin was warm under her fingers as she dressed the wound.

'What happened to your leg?' she asked, eyes flitting over the powerful spread of his shoulders, the way his torso tapered down into a narrow waist and the long, muscular legs covered in curly dark hair and sticking out from under the white towel.

'Training exercise gone wrong. Should be good as new in no time.'

When she didn't say anything, he went on. 'The surgeon cut through a nerve so the skin on the left side of the scar is numb. He said it'll reattach over time and the feeling will come back.'

'Was that your only injury?'

'Pretty much. I was lucky.'

Rhiannon thought about how he'd slammed on the brakes when he'd caught sight of the reflectors on her shoes. Often, the mental scars were worse than the physical.

With a rush of compassion for her old friend, she pulled the towel higher and covered his delightful derriere. 'Has the stinging stopped now?'

'Yeah, it feels good. Thanks.'

'Okay, you can get dressed.'

Rhiannon turned away from the table and peeled off her gloves. While Cameron dressed, she washed and dried her hands then busied herself putting away the mess on the bench and attending to the paperwork.

Then all at once he was standing in front of her, filling the small room, a smile on his lips. 'I'm sorry about before.'

'Think nothing of it.' She handed him a tablet and a glass of water, fingertips tingling as her hands brushed his. 'Swallow this antihistamine. It will take the swelling down and settle the itch.'

He put the tablet in his mouth, studying her face over the rim of the glass as he washed it down.

'How long are you home for?' she asked, taking back the glass.

'For good. I've been discharged.'

Rhiannon smiled. Suddenly, the day took on a rosier hue for knowing Cameron Reid was once again a permanent resident of Bindarra Creek.

'That's happy news, Cameron. Are you pleased about the discharge?'

'I am. It's the right time. The family need me.'

'Of course.' Rhiannon walked to the door and held it open for him. He was leaving one form of duty to take up another. 'Sometimes, you have to know when to walk away from something, don't you?'

'If you're lucky.' His eyes narrowed as if trying to read more into what she was saying.

She held out her hand. She didn't want to say something trite like 'see you soon' or 'catch up with you later'. She'd offered him the chance to reconnect over coffee and he'd declined. 'Bye, Cameron.'

He took her hand in a warm, firm grip and gave it a light squeeze. But instead of releasing her hand he looked down at her wrist.

'How's the Fitbit going?'

'Oh,' Rhiannon withdrew her hand. 'I really like it. I'm using it to monitor my fitness. I've entered a charity mud run that's coming up after Christmas.'

'Ah. Must be a new event on the Bindarra Creek social calendar.'

'Yes. Is that something you'd be interested in? The entry forms are on the reception desk.'

He shook his head and this time he did turn to leave. 'I did that sort of thing as a day job, there's no way I'd do it for pleasure. I'm happy to make a donation though.'

***

What the hell was the matter with him?

Rhiannon was gorgeous! She'd been kind and caring in an awkward situation, though he could have done without her descriptive language like 'engorged' and 'sucking'. His imagination had run riot, his eyes closing, teeth gritting, heart slamming against the examination table, skin turning sensitive at her touch.

He sighed and handed his card to the receptionist. What a pity his first 'up close and personal' encounter with Rhiannon had to be in a sterile doctor's surgery with a paralysis tick for company.

Who's fault was that?

Twice he'd had the opportunity to see her again and twice he'd pushed her away, saying there was no need to come out to the property and declining her offer to have coffee. Now, to top it off, he'd just refused to go in the mud run.

He wouldn't change his mind about the mud run though. He'd army crawled through enough dirt and mud to last him a lifetime, and there was always enough physical work to do on the property. What was wrong with a game of tennis? He'd be up for that once his leg improved.

A purring female voice spoke his name and Cameron turned to see the small figure of Vera Wilson standing behind him. Well into her seventies, it appeared Mrs. Wilson had taken on the mantle of Bindarra Creek's resident cougar. Dressed in tight black pants and a leopard print blouse, she was loaded down with enough bling to attract the magpies. Straight silver hair swung around her chin when she moved.

'Hello, Mrs. Wilson.'

'Call me Vera, sweetie.' She laid a hand on his arm, nails varnished with hot pink lacquer, eyelashes clumped together with a thick coating of charcoal mascara. 'I'm so pleased you're home safely, Cam. I understand you slipped into town without anyone knowing.'

'Dad kept it pretty quiet. He's superstitious that way.'

'Shame on him. I'll have to have a word.'

'Mrs. Wilson, you can come through now.'

Rhiannon was standing in the corridor outside her room.

Go on!

What are you waiting for?

Cameron turned and gave Vera an admiring smile. 'Vera, would you bear with me for a second? I think I've left something in the nurse's room.'

His use of her first name brought a delighted smile to Vera's bright pink lips. 'Of course you can you gorgeous boy. I'm in no hurry.'

Cameron stepped around Vera Wilson and headed up the hallway where Rhiannon had retreated into her room. When he got there, she was looking around searching for the mystery item he'd supposedly lost.

'I can't see anything. What did you forget?'

His heartbeat went into overdrive. 'An invitation.'

She continued looking around the room. 'Is it in an envelope? I don't remember you having it with you when you came in.'

'I didn't. It's a coffee invitation.'

She stilled.

'No, actually, it's for dinner.'

She didn't say anything, just stared at him with those shining brown eyes that had always made him feel like he was the only person in the world worth talking to.

He launched into his spiel before he had a chance to overthink it. 'I think I've given you the wrong impression. I'd love to catch up, but it's been so long, I think we'll need more than coffee. I don't even know what brought you back to Bindarra Creek.'

She nodded. 'I'd like that.'

'Really? If I'm stepping on anyone's toes, just say so.'

'No. There's no-one.'

Cameron dragged in a deep breath and blew it out again. 'Right, I'm glad we got that one sorted. Next question. Where would you like to go? I'm a bit out of the loop.'

'Ah, let's see. There's the Royal pub. The Riverside is closed at the moment. And there's the bowling club.' A frown creased her forehead as she paused to think. 'Oh, we now have an Asian restaurant. I don't think the Cyprus Café opens for dinner.'

'Hmm, not exactly spoilt for choice are we?'

She hesitated then appeared to come to a decision. 'Would you like to come over to my place? I rent May Bannister's granny flat. She lets me make full use of the house.'

'But ... I don't want you to have to cook,' Cameron said, taken aback by the surprise invitation to meet at her place.

Not that he minded.

He didn't mind one little bit.

'The Asian place delivers, and May goes to bed early.' A pink colour rose in her creamy cheeks. 'Don't take this the wrong way but I'd rather not set people's tongues wagging.'

So that was it.

'I know what you mean. There's no anonymity in a small country town.'

'Exactly.'

'And it's natural for people to come up and welcome me home. They're well-meaning but...' He hesitated. They wouldn't have any privacy in a pub or a restaurant.

'So it's your place. How does Saturday at seven work for you?'

'That's perfect.' She smiled. 'I'll look forward to it.'

'Me too. I'll bring wine.' Cameron backed away towards the door, eyes on her, greedy for one last look.

'Go on, soldier,' she said with mock severity. 'I have patients waiting.'

With one last grin, he swaggered off to collect his card from the receptionist.

With a wink at Vera Wilson who was still standing at the reception desk, he pulled his car keys from his pocket, tossed them in the air and caught them again. He knew he had a goofy smile on his face but he didn't care. He had a date with a gorgeous nurse working in his mother's old position at Doc. Warner's.

Maybe his mother was looking down on him after all.

CHAPTER NINE

Cameron lifted the plastic container and began refuelling the Polaris. Behind him, Jed was shuffling around the TD, polishing the duco to a mirror shine. Outside, promising storm clouds obscured the midday sun. The cows and calves Cameron had herded into the top paddock were taking shelter under the trees and settling into their new abode.

Cameron emptied the container and looked at Jed. 'It's about time we fired up Lucille and took her out for a run, Dad.'

An image popped into Cameron's head. He was driving through the countryside, top down, dappled sunlight filtering through the ghost gums. Rhiannon smiled at him from the passenger seat, oversized black sunnies perched on her nose, hair blowing around her face.

'We'll have to do it soon. Show's on in a couple of weeks.'

'The show?' Erasing the image of Rhiannon from his mind, Cameron set the container on the concrete floor. He'd been away so long he'd forgotten about the regional show. 'Are you putting the car in an exhibition?'

Jed snorted. 'I wish! Those blasted women on the CWA cornered me one morning and asked how the restoration was going. I thought they were interested in the car. Should have known they were up to something. When I said it was nearly finished they roped me into driving one of the show girl contestants around the arena. Apparently they're parading them around on vintage cars this year.'

Cameron grinned. The New England regional show was a major highlight on the annual social calendar. 'Where's the harm in that?'

'No harm at all, it doesn't bother me. I'm not allowed to drive remember, so it looks like you're it!'

'*What?*' I have to drive a show girl around?'

'Yep.'

'Oh...'

'If you don't want to do it take it up with Edwina Lette and her cronies on the CWA.'

Cameron pushed his hair back with his fingers. Was this for real? He'd gone from a Special Forces officer to answerable to the Country Women's Association. He was about as far removed from the Middle East as he could get.

Reminding himself that was a good thing, he wiped his hands on a piece of rag. 'It's all good, Dad, I'll do it.

Those CWA ladies are a force to be reckoned with. I'll never hear the end of it if I let them down.'

Jed was enjoying getting some of his own back after their discussion last night. While he hadn't agreed to hand in his license, he'd promised Cameron he wouldn't' drive. It was a step in the right direction. Their appointment with Doc. Warner in a few hours' time was another step.

Cameron threw the rag onto a work bench and rested his hands on his hips. 'We'd better get moving Dad. Pete was good enough to fit you in this afternoon. We don't want to keep him waiting.'

'I'm only doing this to please you kids.'

Cameron frowned. 'Why would you say that? This procedure could improve your quality of life.'

'Humph! Well, I'll listen to what the good Doc has to say. Then I'll make up my own mind.'

Two and a half hours later, Doc. Warner slid a stack of papers into a large, yellow envelope and passed it across the desk to Cameron. 'All the information we've spoken about is in there.'

'Thanks, Pete.'

Doc. Warner shifted his gaze to Jed. 'Take your time and read the literature. Have a think about it, talk it over with Cam and Tori, even get another medical opinion if you like.'

'Why would I do that?' asked Jed. 'You've been my friend and doctor for thirty-five years. I just have to decide whether I trust this mob in Melbourne to do it.'

'Deep brain stimulation is pretty standard these days, and this team are at the top of their field.'

'I still want to know what guarantees they can give me.'

Doc. Warner nodded. 'It's important you're in full possession of the facts, Jed. And you never know, there's a slight chance you mightn't be a good candidate for the procedure.'

'Do you think that's likely?' asked Cameron. He hadn't thought of that.

'In my opinion it's highly unlikely.' Pete Warner spoke to his father again. 'You're suffering side effects from the medication and 'wearing off' spells. That makes you a good candidate for this. When you can turn off the tremors, your balance and movement will improve. You'll become more active, get stronger and build more muscle. The benefits of this procedure can last up to five years.'

Jed tilted his head in Cameron's direction. 'I gave my word to Cam last night that I won't get behind the wheel of a car. I'll give it to you too, Pete. The last thing I want is to be a menace on the roads. Having said that, no-one's talking me into giving up my license. If I hand it in now there's a good chance they won't give it back.'

Cameron held his breath as Pete Warner mulled over Jed's words.

'I suppose there's a risk that could happen.'

'And there's a chance I could drive again if the operation is a success?'

'There's every chance.'

91

'Every chance?' Jed leaned forward in his chair, and though his mask-like expression barely changed, Cameron didn't miss the way his eyes shone with anticipation.

Cameron's heart contracted and he rubbed a hand down his face. His father's body was becoming more and more debilitated, but it was the frozen facial muscles Cameron found difficult to deal with. No matter what Jed was feeling, his face was devoid of expression.

Memories of a younger, fitter Jed slipped into Cameron's mind. The laughter creases in Jed's weathered face as he regaled them with a funny story or cracked up laughing at a trick he'd played on Tori. A contented smile on his lips as he sat astride the chestnut mare they used to own, crow's feet fanning out from the corners of his eyes as he gazed with pride over Bindarra Downs. Jed's tanned face, crumpled in grief at his wife's funeral. The worried frown and absent smile as he'd waved Cameron off to war.

'So, is my word good enough for you, Pete?' Jed was saying. 'I stay off the road and you don't put the form in until I decide whether or not I have the operation?'

'Your word's always been good enough for me, Jed.'

Jed nodded, his gaze sliding to Cameron. 'Righto. I suppose that's it then.'

Both Cameron and Pete Warner stood up. Jed made a couple of attempts before Cameron took hold of his arm and helped him to his feet.

'Ah! The old legs don't work very well these days.'

Pete Warner shook hands with Cameron and then with his father. 'I'm glad you decided to come in, Jed.' Pete opened the door then rested a hand on Jed's shoulder. 'A little way down the track my friend and I think you'll be very pleased you did.'

Outside the surgery, Cameron looked up and down River Road, disappointed he hadn't 'accidentally' run into Rhiannon at the surgery.

Get a grip! You haven't seen her for fifteen years, you can wait another couple of days.

'What do you want to do, Dad? We have an hour and a half until we pick up Tori.'

'The markets are on.'

'Are they still in the same place?' From Cameron's recollection, the council closed off Banksia Street between River Road and Mt. Ingall's Road for the fortnightly markets.

'Yep.'

'Okay, let's check them out, and after that we can grab some lunch at the Royal Pub.'

Cameron matched his stride to Jed's and looked up at the darkening sky. 'Those clouds look promising.'

'The rain will come.' Jed didn't look up, just kept his focus on the pavement ahead of him. 'It always does at this time.'

'I seem to remember it always raining for the show.'

'Nothing surer.' Jed chuckled. 'Those show girls could be under the vinyl roof and no-one will see them.'

Cameron smiled. Jed seemed better today. His stride had lengthened and there'd been no freezing or false starts since leaving home.

'You're walking pretty well at the moment, Dad.'

'So are you!'

Cameron burst out laughing. Jed's body might be failing but his wit was as sharp as ever.

'It's the farm work. What's your reason?'

'The tablets are working on me at the moment.'

Cameron nodded and chose his words carefully, 'When you suffer those 'wearing off' spells Doc. Warner spoke of, I wonder if a walker wouldn't give you more stability.'

Jed gave him a sharp look. 'I don't need one of those.'

They crossed the street and continued onto the next block. 'I'm worried about you falling over, Dad. The hallways at home are six feet wide, plenty wide enough for a walker or even a motorised scooter. I've been thinking about it. There's a lot we can do to make your life easier, like turning the downstairs study into your bedroom so you don't have to climb the stairs.'

'I thought you wanted me to have the operation?'

'I want you to find out everything you can so you can make an informed decision, that's what I want. In the meantime, I think we can make changes which will help.'

'Okay, look mate, I'm sick of talking about myself. Can we just have a look at some of these stalls?'

'Sure.' Cameron looked up as they turned the corner into Banksia Drive. Trestle tables lined both sides of the street, shaded by assorted marquees, sunshades and tarpaulins. Vendors from Bindarra Creek and the surrounding area sat or stood behind tables laden with fresh produce and a variety of homemade jams and preserves like tomato relish and fig jam.

Cameron's gaze swept the area—right to left, left to right, taking note of every bag and backpack, every obstacle, every vehicle parked within a hundred metres of the market. He ran a hand around the back of his neck and reminded himself he wasn't in Iraq.

It didn't help.

His hand came away sweaty and he wiped it down the leg of his jeans. He hated crowds, even small ones like this of 100-150 people max. Covert surveillance, stealth training, camouflage and a controlled approach were his strengths. Wandering around an open air, country market was a simple pleasure that should be enjoyed, but it only brought his training and instincts to the fore.

Only at Bindarra Downs could he truly relax.

'Fancy anything in particular, Dad?' he asked in an effort to distract himself.

Jed pointed to a nearby stall. 'Pick up some of that homemade lemon butter, Cam.'

Cameron paid for two jars, nodded a brief hello to a couple of acquaintances he recognised and then he and Jed walked along to the next stall where an artist was displaying landscapes in a variety of different sizes. Most of the paintings were from the Uralla region and included sites from Captain Thunderbolt's trail.

'They're really good.' Cameron leaned over and took a closer look at a couple of pieces that caught his eye.

Thunderbolt was one of Australia's most notorious bushrangers, responsible for hundreds of armed robberies during the 1800's. 'I like this one of Thunderbolt's rock and this one of his cave.'

'They're not bad,' said Jed. 'I especially like the one of his hideout.'

'I think I'll buy them.' Cameron couldn't remember his father purchasing any new art for the house since his mother died, and after twelve years in Special Forces with little or no expenses he had more money than he knew what to do with. He planned using a large chunk of it to install more irrigation on the property and maybe invest a portion in some Angus cattle.

Cameron reached behind his back for his wallet, watching for any sign that Jed might object to the painting of the rock where the bushranger sat astride a horse.

But Jed said nothing, just looked at each painting in turn.

'I'd rather give my money to this local bloke than some fancy art dealer in Sydney.'

Jed nodded again, eyes on the paintings. 'Where will you hang them?'

'Maybe in the hallway.'

Cameron stilled as over Jed's shoulder he glimpsed Rhiannon. She was standing at a fruit stall on the other side of the road, cords dangling from her ears just like the other morning when he'd come to a screeching halt in the car. But she wasn't listening to music today. She held a mobile phone in one hand and a punnet of strawberries in the other. She was speaking into the tiny microphone attached to the cord dangling beneath her chin, an earnest expression on her face.

Jed turned to see what he was looking at.

'Ah! *Her!*'

Cameron frowned. 'Don't be like that, Dad. Why don't you like her?'

'Who says I don't like her?'

'No-one. It's pretty obvious, that's all.'

Cameron nodded to the artist who was waiting anxiously to see if he'd made a sale.

'I like the girl,' declared Jed. 'She's a sassy little thing from the city—reminds me of your mother.'

'I thought that might be it. It's not that she looks like Mum, but she has the same caring manner.'

'Yeah, always trying to tell me what's best for me.'

Right then Rhiannon turned around, eyes scanning the crowd like she sensed someone watching her.

Jed raised his hand and gave her a friendly wave.

Rhiannon waved back, mobile clutched in her palm.

Jed chuckled. 'I have the ultimate respect for that girl, pulling a tick out of your arse.'

Cameron smiled. 'You'll keep mate, you'll keep.'

Cameron waved back, though he didn't miss how Rhiannon's smile failed to erase the pre-occupied expression in her eyes.

***

Rhiannon broke eye contact with Cameron as the receptionist at Strong Lawyers came on the line.

'Hello, Ms. Scott, Mr. Strong's still busy. Should I have him call you back?'

'No, I'm fine to wait.' She'd been playing telephone tag with her lawyer all morning. His voice message had stressed it was important.

'Putting you on hold.'

Rhiannon clenched her jaw as the irritatingly repetitive sequence of notes began playing again. Over at the artist's stall, Cameron was handing over cash for the purchase he'd made.

'Rhiannon?'

She swung away as her lawyer came on the line. 'Yes, Rick.'

'Thanks for getting back to me. There's been a development at this end.'

Rhiannon walked in the opposite direction from where Jed and Cameron were standing. Head down, so she didn't make eye contact with anyone who could interrupt her, she walked slowly towards Mt. Ingall's Road.

'What kind of development?'

'According to our source, Dominic Mullen's been absent from work for the past four days. He hasn't called in sick or taken leave. He's not answering his phone. They've been unable to contact him or his family. Basically, no-one knows what's going on. People in the hospital are talking abandonment of employment.'

'Has anyone been to the house?' Rhiannon ducked under an awning as cold raindrops splashed onto her bare arms.

'I imagine that would have already happened. Management are being very tight lipped about it. I just wanted to let you know we're monitoring the situation carefully.'

'It's extraordinary.' Rhiannon stared down at the large blocks of sandstone pavement. 'Especially if he's had appointments and deliveries scheduled.'

'Yes. It's like he's just walked away, disappeared into thin air.'

A chill slipped down Rhiannon's spine and she turned and scanned the crowd milling around the markets. 'Do you think he might come here?'

'It did cross my mind.'

'The guy has a cocaine habit, Rick. Who knows what he'll do.'

'Exactly.'

'So, what's the plan now?'

'We wait. The hearing's a month away. Sit tight, and I'll let you know as soon as I hear more from our source. I'm also expecting to hear from his lawyers.'

'Okay.'

'How's things at your end?'

Rhiannon turned and looked to where the artist was handing a wrapped package to Cameron. She'd been thinking about him ever since he'd come into the surgery. With luck, he and Jed would hang around for a bit and she could catch them up when she was done here.

'Someone's watching me. A different guy to the one who came up before. This one's fair, thickset, drives a grey Honda.'

'Has he approached you?'

'No. He saw me take his photo on my phone though. I thought it might frighten him off. I got his number plate. He followed me, high beamed me when I was stopped.'

'Did you report it to the police?'

'I decided not to.'

She took a deep breath and risked another glance at Cameron. He was carrying the wrapped package under his right arm, his left wrapped around Jed's shoulders as they hurried to get out of the rain.

'Give me the registration number,' Rick Strong said.

Rhiannon recited the number she'd committed to memory then waited as her lawyer read it back. 'That's it.'

'I'll see what I can find out.'

'Thanks, Rick.'

'Keep safe, Rhiannon. We're almost there.'

'It's not my safety I'm worried about.' It was the safety of the mothers and babies under the care of Dominic Mullen that kept her awake at night.

'In a few weeks' time you'll be free of that backwater town and have your old life back again. You can put this whole sorry episode behind you.'

Rhiannon bristled and fought off the urge to jump to the town's defence. 'I do miss the midwifery Rick, but honestly, it hasn't been that bad.'

It was true. She was looking forward to working with babies again but she had enjoyed caring for the people of Bindarra Creek. What the town lacked in state of the art facilities it made up for with its personalised care. The maternity suite at the hospital was a transient place. Mums came in, babies were born and after a few days they went home and new families came in. In Bindarra Creek, patient care was ongoing, week after week, month after month, year after year. And in Doc. Warner's case, decade after decade.

She turned to look at Cameron and Jed, disappointed when they turned the corner without a backward glance.

'Keep your phone handy,' Rick Strong was saying. 'Mullen has one more day before he's considered to have abandoned his employment. I'll be in touch the instant we know more.'

CHAPTER TEN

Cameron walked towards the pool of light on May Bannister's porch, leather wine holder swinging from his right shoulder. The cooler section brushed his hip when he moved reminding him of the assault weapon he used to carry. He touched his fingers to the smooth leather. Nothing more lethal inside than a bottle of the Hunter's finest Semillon and another of smooth Shiraz.

He rang the doorbell and listened as the four note sequence reverberated throughout May's house. He had nerves of steel ... normally. He was trained to pull a trigger, to end a life in the blink of an eye. Now, he was standing on a porch, heart rate elevated, hoping those nerves didn't affect his voice the way it did his hands.

The door opened and Rhiannon stood framed in the light from the hallway. She wore close fitting dark blue jeans, a soft white jumper and an agitated expression. She raised both hands, palms towards him like she was about to tell him to go away.

'I'm so sorry, Cameron. Allow me to apologise in advance.'

Not the best start to the evening.

'Okay,' he said, wondering what had got her all worked up.

'It's May.'

'Oh, God! Is she alright?'

Rhiannon shot a glance over her shoulder and pulled the door closed behind her. 'She's in her *element*.'

'I'm sorry, I'm not following you.'

'I know, I'm not making any sense.' She lowered her voice. 'I told May through the week you were coming over. I stressed it was a casual thing and that we were going to order in.' She waved a dismissive hand. 'Anyway, this afternoon I got called into work. When I got home, she was in the kitchen cooking up a feast ... for *us!*'

Cameron expelled a breath. 'Well, that's good, isn't it? I thought you were going to tell me she'd been taken ill.'

'No, but...' Rhiannon gazed up at him with uncertain eyes. 'I wanted to warn you she's got the table set for two like it's a romantic dinner. I don't have the heart to disappoint her, she's been having so much fun. She's going to wait on us as if we were in a restaurant. She's even lit the candles.'

Cameron had to stop himself from laughing. Rhiannon had got herself all worked up over nothing. He reached out and took her by the shoulders, the mohair jumper soft beneath his palms. 'Don't stress. Twelve years of army food and I'll take one of May Bannister's legendary home cooked dinners over takeaway every time.'

She took a deep breath, her shoulders rising beneath his hands. 'Thank you for being so understanding. I'm sorry she's got the wrong idea.'

The wrong idea?

Maybe his idea about tonight was more in keeping with May's than Rhiannon's.

He let go of her shoulders.

Rhiannon shook her head. 'May's a hopeless matchmaker. She can't help herself.'

Rhiannon was a softie. On the one hand she didn't want to hurt May's feelings and on the other hand she was worried what he would think. And May, with her enthusiasm for matchmaking, might have handed him the perfect opportunity to charm the pants off Rhiannon tonight.

Figuratively.

At least at this early stage.

'Well, if May can't help herself, I think we should go inside and do justice to her efforts. There are worse things than being a hopeless matchmaker.'

Rhiannon smiled up at him, brown eyes shining with gratitude and Cameron couldn't help catching his breath.

He held the door for her, and she led the way inside. In the living room, a fire crackled and popped in the grate beneath the mantle. Cole Porter crooned Begin the Beguine from massive speakers attached to an old-fashioned turntable. A fancy lace cloth covered the dining table where two taper candles already burned in golden candlesticks. Two places were set with shining cutlery and crockery with people's faces on it.

Cameron leaned in to take a closer look, the strap sliding off his shoulder and catching at his elbow. 'Is that ... Princess Diana and Charles?'

'Here, let me take that.'

Cameron straightened, skin tingling as she slid the strap down his arm and over his hand. 'Thanks.'

'May's a monarchist. The china cabinets are full of royal family memorabilia.'

'Is that right?' He leaned over and looked at the gold embossed plate. Charles and Diana smiled from inside a red heart. 'His Royal Highness Prince Charles and Lady Diana Spencer,' Cameron read out the words. 'To commemorate their marriage. 29th July, 1981.'

He straightened and turned to face her again. 'Before you and I were born.'

'Yes.' Rhiannon made a face. 'Their marriage didn't end well, did it, and then to be followed by such a tragedy. Anyway...' She lifted the wine cooler. 'I'll take this into the kitchen. Make yourself at home.'

Cameron watched her leave, admiring the sexy dip in her back and the swing of her hips as she walked. He remembered that walk from fifteen years ago, head high, shoulders back as she strutted around the tennis court like she owned it. He hadn't been able to take his eyes off her back then either.

Left alone, he wandered over to study the contents of the mirror backed china cabinet. May really was a royalist judging by the amount of china mugs, cake plates and photo frames that were stacked inside. There were even a few sets of wine glasses and a china thimble.

'It's dangerous now I have access to e-bay,' a voice said from behind him.

He wheeled around to see a smiling May. She was coming towards him, a tiny glass in each hand and he would have bet his life they weren't shots.

'Hello, May.' Cameron leaned over and kissed the older woman on both cheeks, something he'd grown accustomed to while on leave overseas.

She put the glasses down and took him by the shoulders. 'Well now, look at you. All European.'

'I dunno about that.'

'It's good to have you home, Cam,' she said as Rhiannon came back into the room. 'Just as well you have broad shoulders too, with everything you've got on your plate.'

Rhiannon's amused gaze met his over the top of May's head.

'You shouldn't have gone to all this trouble for us. We were going to order Asian.'

May shuddered and picked up the glasses. 'I don't go much on that restaurant. Besides, I like having someone to cook for. Rhiannon prefers to do her own thing. She won't put anything in her mouth that will make her fat.'

'That's not true,' protested Rhiannon. 'I'm just being thoughtful. I don't expect you to cook for me every night.'

Cameron looked on in amusement as May kept talking. 'Always got that thing on her wrist, beeping out how many kilojoules she's burned and how many steps she's taken.' May shook her head. 'I don't know why she bothers, she has a lovely figure, doesn't she, Cameron?'

'May!' Colour rose in Rhiannon's cheeks. 'I ate some of that coconut slice you made last week.'

'As if that little piece will make you fat! Anyway, I have to get back to the kitchen.' She handed each of them a glass. 'Here, you two enjoy a pre-dinner Sherry.'

Cameron's stomach turned over, an image of rotting corpses flashing in his mind's eye.

Christ!

He hated Sherry with a vengeance. He should have brought some beers to drink but he didn't want Rhiannon to think he was some kind of country bogan.

'Thank you.' He took the glass from May, beads of sweat breaking out on his forehead as he watched her leave the room.

'Cheers.' Rhiannon raised her glass and took a small sip. 'Thanks for coming over, Cameron, and thanks for not getting weirded out by all this.'

Stomach muscles contracting, Cameron raised the glass to chin level. Sherry was meant to be sipped but the only way he was going to get this down his gullet was to throw it back like a shot.

He put the glass to his lips, halting as the Sherry's nauseatingly sweet bouquet infiltrated his nostrils.

Shit, not now.

He lowered the glass, went lightheaded as the blood left his face. 'I'm sorry. There's not many things I can't stomach, but sweet Sherry's one of them.'

Rhiannon froze. 'Don't drink it.'

'I don't want to offend her.'

She shook her head. 'Doesn't matter.'

'Is there a bathroom nearby? I could tip it out.'

She didn't answer, just raised her glass and downed its contents.

'Whoa!'

Grimacing, she thrust the empty glass at him. 'Give me the full one.'

Her soft fingertips brushed against the back of his hand as they swapped glasses, the contact grounding him.

He gazed down at the empty glass in his hand and pulled in a long, deep breath. She'd think him a right wuss, sickened by something as harmless as a glass of Sherry.

'Feel better?'

'Yeah, thanks.'

'Odours are the worst, especially sweet ones. It's the whole rotting flesh thing.'

'You got it.'

Relief washed over him. She understood. Perhaps it was the nurse in her, though he'd met many a nurse over the years who lacked Rhiannon's empathy.

'Anyway,' she went on. 'You're driving, aren't you? Save one of your standard drinks for something you enjoy.'

He smiled, appreciating the effort she was making to distract him from the images associated with the aroma. 'I like your thinking.'

He liked more than her thinking. He liked the way she looked, how she spoke, the kindness in her eyes. When they were teenagers they'd had this comfortable way between them, teasing, laughing ... and caring too, in an adolescent way. He'd assumed he'd have a similar rapport with every girl he met, but it wasn't to be. Not that he'd dated much in the army. No point getting serious when you couldn't guarantee you'd survive the next mission.

'What brought you back here?'

'You mean you haven't heard?' Her voice turned low. 'I thought you would have asked someone.'

'I'm asking now.'

She shifted her gaze towards the fire, bluey grey eyeshadow giving her eyes a smoky look. He could watch her for ages, the movement of her shiny hair, the smear of pink lip gloss she left on the rim of her glass.

'A scandal. I ran away from a scandal in the city.'

Cameron frowned. The Rhiannon Scott he remembered would never have run from anything. 'You don't have to talk about it if you don't want to.'

Had he said that for her sake or his? Maybe he didn't want his image of 'the perfect Rhiannon' tainted by the reality of the intervening years.

She paused as May came into the room carrying a bottle of red wine. May filled the Charles and Diana glasses almost to the rim then left as quickly as she'd come.

'Let's talk about you, Cameron. I'm sure your life's been far more exciting than mine.'

'That would be a quick conversation. Special Forces can't talk details, just general stuff.'

'That must be difficult.'

'Women usually find me one of two things, depending on their perspective. Either I'm a fantastic listener or boring as all hell.'

She smiled. 'I can't imagine anyone finding you boring.'

His heart skipped a beat. The truth was, with most women he'd met while on leave he couldn't be bothered putting in the effort.

'Normally, I don't talk about what brought me back,' she said. 'I end up boring myself.'

She took another sip of Sherry, the glass clutched between slim, delicate fingers. 'Still, I'd rather you hear it from me than somebody else. Did you know I'm a midwife?'

Cameron shook his head. 'I thought you were a general nurse.'

'In Bindarra Creek I am, though I've been lucky enough to deliver a few babies while I've been here.'

He nodded. He could see her doing that.

'So, you didn't follow in your father's footsteps and become a doctor after all?'

'You have a good memory. No, I didn't want to do the medicine thing. I love babies.'

A rush of testosterone hit him like freight train. He wanted to tell her he loved babies too, that he'd adored Tori from the moment his mother had brought her home from hospital.

'Before I came here I was working at the Royal Mercy Hospital, mostly for a young, gifted obstetrician.'

An affair?

Was that the scandal?

Cameron held his breath.

'He started making mistakes, which was unusual.' She gazed into the fire, eyes lost in the past. 'He began dropping things, then progressed to errors of judgment. I thought he was overtired. We'd had a run of late night deliveries and the doctors' schedules are always gruelling. Then one night, he failed to stem a mother's blood loss after a difficult birth. If I hadn't been there...'

Cameron expelled his breath. 'You saved the woman's life?'

'And saved him from a malpractice suit.' She reached up and put her Sherry on the mantelpiece. 'Afterwards, I went into his office. I was so worried and upset I walked straight in without knocking. There were two lines of white powder on the desk in front of him.'

Cameron closed his eyes. It was a familiar story and yet it never failed to shock him. How many men in the armed forces had turned to drugs to cope? And the outcomes were horrific. At best they earned a dishonourable discharge, which left them with no support—at worst, they let the man beside them down or became a suicide statistic.

He opened his eyes. 'Cocaine?'

'We think so, but I'm the only one who saw it and I can't be sure. I told him he had to get help. I said I'd give him the chance to report it, otherwise I'd do it.'

'Sounds like Dad's situation.'

She nodded. 'Similar. Dominic was very contrite at the time. He told me he'd address the situation.'

'And he didn't, otherwise you wouldn't have ended up here.'

'The next morning he ... he reported me, said I'd made sexual advances towards him in his office following the delivery. I was in shock and ... and stunned. I got hauled up before the hierarchy. I told them the truth and they said they'd look into it. They fired me.'

For a few moments Cameron was lost for words at the injustice of it all. 'That's a terrible story. I'm surprised you didn't take a harder line with my father after that.'

'That was Doc. Warner's call, and Jed's not a desperate addict.'

Still, he could have killed someone, Cameron thought, relieved to have his father's driving problem crossed off his list. 'Go on. I want to hear the rest.'

She drew in a big breath as if to steady herself. 'Every hospital I approached shut the door in my face. I ended up here, where they're so desperate for health workers they'll take anyone.'

There was a sudden rawness to her, and Cameron had to fight the impulse to reach out and drag her into his arms. 'Not anyone, Rhiannon. Doc. Warner's an experienced GP. He's knows a good nurse when he sees one.'

She smiled a little, gratitude mixing with the doubt clouding her eyes. 'Thank you, Cameron.'

An experience like that was sure to have rocked her confidence, in both the system and in the people she trusted. Cameron clenched his jaw. He wanted to ask where her family and friends were in all of this. So far, she hadn't mentioned them.

He leaned closer. 'Sydney's loss is Bindarra Creek's gain.'

It sounded lame, and he doubted his words would help, but the people of this town cherished their medical staff. They'd looked up to his mother, the same way they looked up to Doc. Warner, the same way they looked up to him for fighting for their country.

Old values.

Good values.

Rhiannon would be appreciated in such a community.

She swallowed. 'I'm suing Dominic Mullen for defamation of character and I have an unfair dismissal case against the hospital.'

'Good!'

'The case is up for hearing in a month. If I win, they'll have to reinstate me.'

'And you'd go back after the way they treated you?'

She frowned. 'I deserve to have my reputation restored.'

'Of course you do, and you will, if you win. But the hospital hung you out to dry. They supported the person in the position of power.

She raised a cynical eyebrow. 'Isn't that how things work, Cameron?'

'They don't have to.'

'That's why I need to persist with it. No one is above the law even those who believe they are entitled.'

'I agree...'

'Righto you two, come and sit down!'

Cameron swung around to see May standing in the doorway holding a tray. 'Here, May, let me help you with that.'

'No, no, sit down. I'll put it on the sideboard.'

Needing to do something, Cameron moved over to the table and held a chair out for Rhiannon. He was amazed at her stoicism. It would have been so easy to become consumed by bitterness, fuelled by the injustice of it all. But she'd made a healthy decision and returned to a place that held happy memories for her. She'd got on with her life, found a job, made friends.

Did he form part of those happy memories?

He hoped so.

The girl he'd known back then had blossomed into a fascinating woman and despite her intention to return to Sydney, he really hoped she wouldn't.

CHAPTER ELEVEN

'This looks absolutely delicious, May!' Rhiannon gazed down at the rack of beef ribs and assorted vegetables skilfully arranged on her dinner plate.

Beaming like a lighthouse, May stepped back from the table and wiped her hands on her Queen Elizabeth Royal Jubilee apron. 'We're in cattle country. Ribs are appropriate.'

'They smell magnificent.' Cameron picked up his fork. 'Do you mind me asking what the thick, dark glaze is?'

'It looks likes molasses, doesn't it?' May planted her hands on her hips. 'It's Jack Daniels and Coca-Cola.'

Cameron grinned. 'What an awesome combination.'

'Try it,' May urged.

Rhiannon watched as Cameron picked up his knife and cut into the rack. He was being such a good sport about all this, and he was so nice to May, Rhiannon could actually believe he was enjoying himself. But that was to be expected, wasn't it? Everybody knew everybody in

Bindarra Creek, and May had known the Reid family for six decades.

Cameron slid a piece of beef into his mouth, his handsome face a picture of concentration. He stared at the tablecloth and chewed the meat slowly like a judge on a cooking show.

'Good flavour, tender.' He glanced at May. 'Black Angus?'

'Yes.'

He nodded. 'It's good. I'm going to look over some steers at the show, and some horses.' He dragged his linen napkin from one of May's royal crown napkin rings and wiped his mouth.

'Horses?' May's eyebrows shot up. 'Good luck with getting that past Jed.'

'It's time.' He pointed his fork at the ribs. 'That glaze is magnificent, May.'

'I might give you the secret recipe one day,' she said, leaving the room with a smile so brilliant she could have just accomplished her life's ambition.

Rhiannon lifted her glass and sipped the wine. 'The Shiraz is good, Cameron.'

'I picked it up in Armidale.'

'Oh?'

'I had to take the Toyota back to the rental company. Angus McGregor's been going back and forth a bit so I hitched a ride home with him.'

'I knew it didn't come from the bottlo at the pub.' Rhiannon took another sip. 'I worked my way through their limited selection months ago.'

His well-shaped lips curved in a smile as he picked up his glass and tasted it as well. 'Hmm. We won't say anything to May, but it's a vast improvement on the Sherry. I'm glad you like it.'

'I do.'

And she liked him.

Rhiannon's blood heated in her veins at the memory of him tasting her lips the way he'd just tasted the wine. What would it be like to kiss him now they were older? Different? Better?

She forced her mind back to the conversation. 'You were talking about the horses. I noticed they were gone when I first went out to Bindarra Downs.'

'Dad got rid of them after Mum died ... and the dogs.'

Rhiannon's heart constricted at the note of desolation in his voice. 'I only met her that one time. She was so lovely. Miriam Jacobs told me it was a riding accident.'

Cameron nodded. 'First ride after having Tori. The kelpie lunged at a wallaby, the mare shied ... Mum came off.'

'I'm so sorry, Cameron.'

He took a deep breath and cut into a baked potato. 'It was a long time ago. I was lucky. I had fifteen years with an incredible mother. Tori has no memory of her.'

Rhiannon watched Cameron as he continued with his meal. He had a habit of putting his cutlery down between every mouthful and eating slowly, something she found surprising for a soldier. Manners instilled by his mother maybe?

'So you think it's time for Bindarra Downs to have dogs and horses again?'

'It's something I feel strongly about, not that Tori will ever ride a horse if Dad has anything to do with it.'

'Jed must have been grief stricken to get rid of the horses like that. You had quite a few from memory.'

'I never agreed with Dad replacing the working animals with trail bikes and the Polaris. Mum loved those horses. She would never have wanted that. It was a freak accident.'

'People cope with grief in different ways. They do whatever they need to do to get through it.'

'I understand now, but at the time all I knew was that I'd lost my mother, my father was barely existing and our beloved animals had been taken away too. After three years I couldn't take it anymore. Dad had employed a nanny for Tori so I left and joined the army. Dad didn't agree with that decision. We were hardly speaking when I left.'

'Really? I can't imagine that from what I've seen of the two of you together. How long did that last?'

'Only a few weeks.' He gave a casual shrug. 'We love each other. We couldn't stay mad for long.'

It was nice to hear a man, a hardened soldier, speak in such a loving way about his family.

'He'd lost his wife, it was understandable he'd be terrified of losing his son. You're a tight unit, you three.'

'We always have been. Anyway, enough about us, what about your family?'

Rhiannon started to reply, then stifled a laugh as she was hit by a sudden thought.

'What.' He grinned and picked up his wine glass.

'In keeping with this formal dinner, our conversation has turned typically 'first date'. Soon we'll be asking each other what kind of music we like.'

'What kind of music *do* you like?' he asked, completely deadpan.

She grinned. 'Chilli Peppers. You?'

'John Williams.'

'The composer?'

He nodded. 'I like cinematic music scores.'

'And John Williams in particular?'

'You can't beat Indiana Jones.'

He looked a bit like Indiana himself. When he moved, she caught a glimpse of black cord at his neck and wondered what hung from the end of it. Dog tags? No, they hung from a chain and the SAS weren't allowed to wear anything that identified them.

He winked. 'Next question?'

'I have a hundred things I want to ask you,' she said, then immediately regretted it. It was wrong to start flirting with him when she was leaving town. She had to remember this was supposed to be two old friends catching up.

Just then May appeared in the doorway. 'How is everything?'

Cameron leaned back in his chair, picked up his wine glass and studied Rhiannon's face. 'It's beautiful, Mrs. B.

Only to be surpassed by the beauty of my two companions.'

As heat rose in Rhiannon's cheeks, May came further into the room and made a shooing motion with her hand. 'Oh, go on with you. You haven't called me Mrs. B. since I worked on the school canteen.'

'I seem to remember the food being better on the days when you were rostered on.'

'You always were a bit of a charmer, Cam.'

Rhiannon swivelled around in her seat. 'May, please come and join us. Don't eat out in the kitchen by yourself.'

'I've finished mine.' She picked up the wine bottle and topped up their glasses. 'Don't mind me, you two take your time, you've got a lot to catch up on. I've made a pavlova so there's no worries about it going cold.'

As May left, Rhiannon picked up her knife and fork again. The meal was delicious but the butterflies in her stomach were suppressing her appetite. All the time she'd lived and worked in Sydney, she'd never met anyone like Cameron Reid. Come to think of it, she'd never met anyone like him when she'd lived in London for a year either.

'Do your parents get up here very often?' Cameron asked, cutting into another piece of rib.

'You've got to be kidding.' The words were out before she could stop them.

He looked up, a glint of steel in his eyes.

Oh God! He'd taken it the wrong way.

She rushed to explain. 'I didn't mean they won't come here because it's-'

'A boring backwater?'

'No, don't say that. They're embarrassed, Cameron.'

'So am I! It's criminal how this place has been allowed to go to rack and ruin.'

'You've got the wrong idea. It's me ... *I* embarrass them.'

His eyes narrowed and he stared at her as if he couldn't believe what he was hearing.

Rhiannon hastened to explain. 'Mum's okay, although she does subscribe to the school of thought that ...' Rhiannon put her knife and fork on her plate and made quotation marks in the air. 'Doctors are Gods. They should never be challenged in any way. And Dad, well, he's convinced that suing a member of the medical profession is never warranted.'

'Clearly they don't agree with what you've done?'

She shook her head, knowing he would find her family difficult to understand. The Scott's were nothing like the Reid's.

An enormous gust of wind cut off their conversation, rattling the panes of glass in the wooden windows and rustling the trees outside. Heavy raindrops splattered against the glass and a lace curtain billowed into the room.

Cameron slid back his chair. 'I'll get it.'

'Here comes the rain!' May bustled through the doorway, coming to a halt in the middle of the room when she saw Cameron closing the window. 'I know we need it badly but why does it always have to rain for the show?'

'Next weekend's supposed to be fine, I checked,' put in Rhiannon, grateful the awkward conversation about her parents had been short-circuited. 'I'm on call Saturday morning in case the St. John's Ambulance people need me.'

'Well, I hope the forecasters are right this time,' grumbled May. 'It'll be a first if they are.' She dug into her apron and thrust a mobile phone at Rhiannon. 'You left this in the kitchen. It's rung three times. Maybe you should check it.'

'Oh.' Rhiannon took the phone, conscious of Cameron's eyes on her as he came back to the table.

She held up the phone. 'Would you excuse me for a moment? I should listen to this voice mail. I've been expecting a call.'

'Go ahead. I'll help May clear these plates.'

Rick Strong worked obscene hours and it wouldn't surprise her if her lawyer was working on a Saturday night. Yesterday, he'd called to say Dominic Mullen had finally got in contact with the hospital. He'd requested three weeks compassionate leave—for family reasons. According to Rick's sources, no-one at the hospital knew what was going on.

Rhiannon began dialling into her message bank. Her superiors had chosen to believe Dominic Mullen over her but they'd have to be suspicious by now, especially if more complaints had been lodged since they'd fired her.

Rick Strong had suspicions they were moving to cover their own back.

The landline rang.

'I'll get it,' May called from the hallway, shouting to be heard over the loud drumming of rain on the roof tiles.

The warmth of the fire beckoned and Rhiannon gravitated towards it, turning up the volume on her phone as the heavens opened and the guttering began overflowing.

She was listening to the computerised voice telling her there were three new messages in her message bank when May came hurrying into the room, Cameron right behind her.

'Lovey, they need you over at the Porter's place. Suellen's gone into labour. They've been trying to contact you.'

Rhiannon hit the end button and slipped the phone into her pocket. 'Did they say how far apart the contractions are coming?'

'No. It's been fast apparently. They said for you to come as quickly as you can.' May wrung her hands. 'Oh dear, listen to that rain.'

'I'll drive,' said Cameron. 'My car's outside and I know where the Porter's live.'

'Thanks, I'll grab my coat.' Rhiannon shot him a grateful look. She'd be over the driving limit thanks to the two extra sherries.

'I'll get a couple of umbrellas.' May called over her shoulder as she scurried from the room. 'By the sound of that downpour you're going to need them.'

CHAPTER TWELVE

The umbrellas blew inside out the moment Rhiannon and Cameron took the first step off May's verandah.

'Leave them here.' Cameron's shout was almost lost on the howling wind as he took the umbrella from her and dumped it on the porch alongside his.

Head down, Rhiannon descended the four steps, trying to hold the flapping sides of her trench coat together. At the bottom, the wind knocked her sideways and she stumbled off the path, icy rain stinging her cheeks, hair whipping around her face like clothes in a spin cycle.

A hand clamped around her upper arm, righting her. Then a strong arm came around her waist and she was drawn close into Cameron's side. She opened her mouth to say thanks but the wind stole her breath and she struggled for air.

She stumbled towards the car, hand clutching Cameron's jacket, the sodden grass squelching beneath her shoes. The Range Rover's lights flashed as Cameron hit the remote fob and then he was wrenching open the door. 'Climb in.'

She reached for the grab handle, strong hands gripping her waist as he gave her a boost. Then she was inside, hair plastered to her head, coat dripping water onto the seat and floor. Seconds later, he was in the driver's seat, slamming the door closed and grinning at her as he started the engine.

'Okay?'

'Oh. My. *God!*' She shook droplets of rainwater off her hands and began to laugh.

'Isn't this bloody fantastic?' He raked long fingers through his sodden hair, pushing it back from his forehead. 'Twenty mills in about twenty minutes I'd say. Let's hope it keeps up.'

Rhiannon watched as he turned the wipers on and they automatically increased to top speed. He looked like a carefree fifteen year old again, energised at being caught in the rain and rejoicing in the downpour that would go a long way towards easing the drought.

'Thank you for driving me.' A shiver rolled through her body. 'I'm not even sure where the house is.'

He turned the heater on high then reached over and pressed another button on the console. 'I'll put the seat warmer on, not that it'll do much good. By the time it warms up we'll be there.'

Rain blew in horizontal sheets, filling up the potholes in the road so they resembled ocean rock pools. Rainwater raged in the gutters, drains unable to clear the water fast enough so the overflow formed mini fountains at intervals down the street.

Rhiannon clicked in her seatbelt as Cameron pulled away from the curb. 'No matter how uncomfortable we are, it's nothing compared to what's in store for Suellen if she's in labour.'

Five minutes later they pulled up in front of the Porter house. Suellen's mother had turned on the outside light and was waiting just inside the front door.

'Oh thank God you're here. It happened so suddenly. One minute she was fine, the next her waters broke and the contractions began with a vengeance.'

'How far apart are they?'

'I'm not sure ... seconds I think.'

'Seconds?' Rhiannon strode down the hallway. 'Where is she, Mrs. Porter?'

'In her room. Second door on the left.'

'Does she have the urge to push?'

'Yes, but we told her not too. I can't believe how quickly it happened. I had to be induced with my two girls.'

Rhiannon knocked and opened the door, Mrs. Porter on her heels. Suellen was propped up on pillows in a half sitting, half laying position. Perched on the side of the bed was another girl who resembled Suellen enough to be her sister.

'This is my other daughter, Louisa,' said Mrs. Porter.

Rhiannon nodded to the other girl. 'How close are the contractions?' she asked, picking up Suellen's wrist and silently counting along with her pulse.

'I'm hardly getting a break.' Suellen's voice was a whisper, her face slick with perspiration.

Rhiannon let go of Suellen's wrist and spoke to the terrified teenager. 'I need to see how far dilated you are. I'm going to lift up your nightdress.'

Suellen didn't reply, just screwed up her face as another violent contraction gripped her body.

Rhiannon lifted the girl's nightie and stared at a fully dilated cervix. As Suellen's body clenched in a contraction, the baby's head became visible.

Rhiannon straightened. 'Okay, Suellen, you're going to be a new mum very soon.' She took hold of the girl's hand again and gave what she hoped was a reassuring squeeze. 'Now, when the next contraction comes, I want you to bear down as hard as you can and push.'

Suellen slumped back on the pillows, tears forming at the corners of her eyes. 'I can't ... I can't ...'

'Yes, you can.' Rhiannon spoke over her shoulder. 'Mrs. Porter, get Cameron Reid in here. There's no time to get her to the polyclinic. She'll be delivering here.'

Mrs. Porter ran from the room returning ten seconds later with Cameron in tow.

'Okay.' Rhiannon kept hold of Suellen's hand as another contraction rolled through the girl's body. 'That's it. Now push!'

The girl bore down, her entire body tightening as every molecule of energy was used in an effort to push the baby out.

'Mrs. Porter, bring me a basin of warm water and a basin of cold. Also, a few washcloths. Louisa, put a soft sheet and a couple of towels in the clothes dryer to warm them up. Not too hot though.'

'Oh no, oh no,' Suellen screamed as another contraction rolled through her body.

'That's it, bear down, bear down.' Rhiannon peered between the girl's legs. The baby's head appeared. She caught a glimpse of black hair for a second or two and then it receded along with the contraction.

'Can't you give her something?' demanded Louisa, backing away from the bed.

'It's too late for pain relief. Will you put those things in the dryer please?' She glanced over her shoulder. 'Cameron?'

He was beside her in an instant. 'What can I do?'

Calm, no panic, just a wonderfully reassuring 'can do' attitude.

'She's backing up the bed, trying to get away from the pain. How strong's your shoulder?'

'Pretty strong.'

'Good. Sit on the bed.'

He sat without question.

'Take her foot and put her arch against your shoulder. She needs something to push against.'

Rhiannon moved to the head of the bed. 'Suellen, listen to me. Settle your foot into Cameron's shoulder. Bend your leg up.'

The girl did as she was asked and Rhiannon guided her foot into the correct position. 'We're going to use Cameron's shoulder like a stirrup. When the next contraction comes, I want you to push your foot against his shoulder as hard as you can and try to push the baby out.'

She glanced at Cameron. 'You up for this?'

He nodded. 'Sure.'

Suellen began whimpering, head lolling about on the pillow as another strong contraction began almost immediately.

'Cameron, brace yourself.'

Rhiannon got right up in Suellen's face. The girl was overtaken by pain, her body beyond her control. Breathing, meditation, nothing could help her now except her own strength.

'Suellen, grit your teeth and push.'

Suellen pushed, her accompanying bellow drowning out the torrential downpour as it clattered onto the Porter's wrought iron roof.

'That's it. Push against Cameron's shoulder. Come on.'

Body charged with adrenaline, Rhiannon checked on the baby. The tiny head was almost crowning. One more push and the head would be born.

'Push Suellen, push! You're almost there, sweetheart.'

Dear God, don't make there be any complications.

Dear God, don't make the cord be around the neck.

Dear God, don't make the baby be oxygen deprived.

The child was her priority at this point. She had to catch the baby, protect the child's head.

Suellen was on her own.

Except she wasn't. Cameron was there. Rhiannon couldn't hear what he was saying over the blood pounding in her temples, but he was murmuring quiet sounds of encouragement.

And it helped.

Suellen calmed a little.

Rhiannon risked a glance. Cameron's shoulder was thrust forward counteracting the force of Suellen's pushes, like a rugby player bracing for a hit from an opposition forward. Both hands were wrapped around Suellen's lower leg, keeping her foot in place as he encouraged her to bear down harder.

And then with one final roar from Suellen, the baby's head was born.

Rhiannon cradled the head in her hands, quickly checking the mouth with her finger to make sure there wasn't any mucus blocking the throat. 'That's it, that's the head. One more push Suellen and it's over. Come on, one more.'

Then suddenly Rhiannon was holding a slippery, squawking baby in her hands. 'Can I have that warm towel please?'

Carefully, she lifted the baby and laid him tummy down on Suellen's chest. 'Congratulations. You have a baby boy.'

'Oh, my God, is he alright?' Puffing from the exertion, every freckle standing out on her reddened face, Suellen lifted her head and gazed down at her newborn child.

'He's weeks premature as we know,' Rhiannon spread the warm towel over the baby's body. 'But to my eye he looks a reasonable weight. We'll have to get him to the premmie unit in Armidale though.'

'A boy?' Suellen laid a gentle hand on her baby's back. 'I can't believe it. Thank you.'

'You did all the hard work,' said Rhiannon, though she could have sworn she'd run a marathon herself. 'Mrs. Porter, wipe Suellen's face with a cold washcloth could you?'

'Of course. Look this way, darling.'

While Mrs. Porter tended to her daughter, Rhiannon took a warm sheet from Louisa and quickly wrapped the baby in it, cord and all. The rest they'd tend to later when the paramedics turned up.

Finally, she turned and looked at Cameron. He was moving away from the bed, making room for Mrs. Porter and Louisa.

'Thank you.' Suellen smiled at him. 'I hope I didn't hurt you.'

'Always happy to lend a shoulder,' he said with a smile. 'Congratulations. The little bloke's got a scream like Jimmy Barnes.'

Suellen laughed, and a warm sensation rolled through Rhiannon's body. Cameron was so natural, his easygoing comment erasing any semblance of embarrassment the young girl may have felt at his presence.

Rhiannon was about to go over to him when Louisa jumped up. The girl put her hands on his shoulders, stood on tiptoes and kissed him on the cheek. 'Thank you so much!'

'Me? Your sister and Nurse Scott did all the work.'

'You were a great help,' Louisa said a little breathlessly. 'I can't believe I'm an auntie.'

Rhiannon hadn't taken much notice of Louisa, all of her attention had been on her patient. But now, as she left mother and baby to bond for a few moments, she could see that the girl was beautiful. Taller and slimmer than Suellen, she had bone structure that could have been hand drawn, her long strawberry blonde hair swept upwards and secured with a silver clip before falling in a thick tail to the centre of her shoulder blades.

Rhiannon's tummy muscles twisted into a disappointed little knot at the sparkle in Cameron's eyes.

'Well, congratulations Louisa, I'm sure you'll make a stellar auntie, and congratulations to you too Mrs. Porter on becoming a grandmother.'

Hand resting on the doorknob, he took one more look at Louisa then finally turned to Rhiannon. 'Let me know if there's anything else I can do.'

***

An hour and a half later, Cameron stood holding a golf umbrella over Rhiannon. Two paramedics were loading a stretcher bearing Suellen and the baby into the back of an ambulance for transportation to Armidale Hospital.

'Bye, Rhiannon,' called Suellen from inside the ambulance. 'Thanks for everything.'

Rhiannon walked over to the ambulance and leaned inside. 'I'm sure everything's going to be fine.' She grinned at Doc. Warner's receptionist. 'Anyway, you got your wish.'

'What do you mean?'

'You worked right up until the baby was born.'

Suellen laughed and then Mrs. Porter climbed into the back of the ambulance and the paramedics rushed to close the doors against the pouring rain. A few minutes later, the vehicle pulled away from the curb, red light flashing like a beacon in the storm.

Cameron stepped forward and held the umbrella over Rhiannon again. 'Come on Nurse Scott, let's get you home, you're soaked through.'

She pushed back her wet hair with a weary sigh and waved at Louisa who was behind the wheel of a small hatchback. 'I'm glad Louisa's following the ambulance, she can bring her mother home once Suellen and the baby are settled.'

'Will you stop worrying?' He took her arm and together they walked towards the Range Rover. 'Your work is done. You'll be in hospital yourself if you don't get dry.'

'What about you? You're as soaked as I am.'

'I'm used to being wet through and sleeping rough.' He closed the umbrella and helped her into the Range Rover. 'On the other hand, it's good practice for the mud run you've entered.'

Moments later he was climbing into the driver's seat.

'I don't want to think about the mud run now.' She turned to look at him as he started the car and pulled away. 'I just want to get out of these clothes.'

He took his eye off the road and glanced at her. She was huddled in the seat, arms wrapped around her middle, a hands-on nurse who cared for her patients above everything else. And she looked beautiful to him, even with running mascara and wet, bedraggled hair.

Who cared for Rhiannon?

Suddenly Cameron wanted to, and not just as someone he'd had a teenage fling with once, or as a small town acquaintance. As something more.

He braked at a four way stop sign, yielding to a car on his right. The car came slowly, crossing the intersection in front of them.

'Oh no,' Rhiannon murmured. 'Not him again.'

Cameron glanced at her. 'Who?'

'The guy in that car.' She pointed after the Honda. 'He's been following me, I'm sure of it. I gave his number to my lawyer the other day after he high beamed me. My lawyer's looking into it.'

Cameron's blood turned cold in his veins. That car had been parked in the school car park the other day when he'd gone to pick up Tori. He'd noticed Rhiannon looking at it. 'Have you reported it to the police?'

She shook her head and leaned back in the seat. 'Dominic Mullen sent someone up here shortly after I arrived trying to convince me to drop the case. I refused and they went away. I think the guy in the Honda has been sent here to try and unsettle me with his presence, probably a last ditch effort to get me to drop the suit before it goes to court.'

'Jesus! Who are these people? Rhiannon, you have to be careful.'

'I *am* careful. That's why I asked you over to May's tonight. I wasn't worried about the locals seeing us, I was worried about that guy seeing me out with you. My lawyer told me to be discreet.'

Troubled by her story, Cameron accelerated, as much as he dared to in the bad conditions. He gripped the steering wheel tighter and thought about what she'd said. It was entirely plausible that intimidation was the motivation behind this man's presence, and that was a serious enough offence. But 'accidents' had been known to happen before cases made it to court. And Rhiannon was a young woman on her own.

Unable to stop himself, he leaned over and took hold of her hand. She gave him a tired smile and curled icy fingers around his.

Cameron's heart squeezed in his chest. She'd been incredible tonight, calm and competent, issuing orders when warranted and encouraging the expectant mother without raising undue alarm.

But now she was worried and exhausted, thanks to a post adrenaline crash coupled with the physical strain her body was under to maintain its temperature. To add to her worries, the man in the Honda was out on the prowl on a night like tonight.

A short time later, Cameron pulled into the curb outside May Bannister's house. He scanned the waterlogged street for any sign of the grey Honda but everything looked exactly as it had earlier on.

Sick in the guts at the thought of something bad happening to Rhiannon, he killed the engine and hopped out of the Range Rover. The quicker she got inside and warmed up in a hot shower the better.

As for the arsehole in the Honda, he'd be on his way back to Sydney before he knew what hit him.

CHAPTER THIRTEEN

May met them at the front door, wrapped in a woolly pink dressing gown. 'Oh my Lord, look at you two. Come in and get dry for goodness sake. I've been so worried I haven't been able to sleep.'

'Rhiannon needs a hot shower.' Cameron put his hand in the centre of Rhiannon's back and propelled her forward. 'I'm worried she's got hypothermia.'

Rhiannon rolled her eyes at Cameron as they pulled off their shoes and socks and left them at the front door. 'I'm a nurse. I'm not hypothermic.'

May touched Rhiannon's cheek and gave a gasp. 'Oh my, you're freezing lovey.'

'Any pain in the extremities?' Cameron couldn't help asking.

'No, they're just stiff and cold.'

'As are your lips. They have no colour. Now get going.'

'You're as wet as I am,' she said, flinging the words over her shoulder as she crossed the living room.

May gave him a wink. 'Don't worry about Cameron, I'll look after him.'

'I'm not worried,' came Rhiannon's disgruntled voice followed by the sound of a door slamming.

'Do you think she's alright?' May asked, helping him pull off his saturated jacket.

'I think she's just overtired. It's been a stressful night and it's bloody miserable out there.'

'Has Suellen had the baby?'

He nodded. 'About ten minutes after we got there. We just made it.'

'Oh, Lord.' May pointed to his sopping wet shirt. 'Take that off too.'

'It's alright.'

'No it's not, you're dripping all over my carpet.'

'Oh, sorry.' Cameron raked his hair out of his eyes and began unbuttoning his shirt.

'Give it all to me, Cam, and I'll put it in the dryer.'

He handed May the dripping garment, angling his body away as he moved further into the living room. A few jagged scars on his torso weren't able to be explained away as easily as he would have liked.

'What did she have?'

'Huh?'

'*Suellen!*'

'Oh, a boy.' He'd been thinking about Rhiannon. He didn't want to go. He needed to make sure she was okay.

'Mother and baby well?'

May would have made a good detective with her persistent line of enquiry. 'Rhiannon seems to think so, though the baby was a bit early. They're being taken into Armidale as we speak.'

'Well, I'm relieved. I'll be back in a minute, Cam. Stand there in front of the fire.'

Deciding to do as he was told, Cameron turned his back to the warmth and thought about the first time he'd laid eyes on Rhiannon after coming home. He'd scared her that morning, when he'd pulled up suddenly in the car. Her body language as she'd crossed the street told him she was fearful and on edge, and he hadn't even known at the time it was her. And later, on the verandah at home, he'd asked what had brought her back to Bindarra Creek. She'd brushed the question aside and said she'd tell him when he had a week, indicating it was a long story.

But never in his wildest dreams, and he'd had his fair share of those, would he have guessed how complicated her story would be.

Still, he was pleased she trusted him enough to confide in him.

Five minutes later, May was back, scurrying into the room with a blanket, a dry towel and two ominous glass tumblers.

Sending up a silent prayer it wasn't a triple Sherry, Cameron took the blanket and wrapped it around his shoulders, grateful for both its warmth and the cover it offered.

'Here.' May handed him a glass and put the second one down on the coffee table. 'I've made you both a rum toddy. That'll put the fire in your belly.'

Cameron began towelling his hair dry. 'May, you're the woman of my dreams.'

'Oh, go on with you.' She shook her head at him. 'Do you want to have a shower too?'

'No thanks, I've warmed up already. I'll just hang around and make sure Rhiannon's okay.'

'I'm fine.'

He emerged from under the towel to see Rhiannon standing in the doorway, face rosy and free of make-up, wet hair combed straight back from her face. She wore a soft grey tracksuit and pink Ugg boots that made him smile.

'Nice Uggs.'

She came into the room, eyes skimming over him. 'Nice bed hair.'

Their eyes meshed.

Cameron's heart pumped.

'Well I'm going to love you and leave you.' May waved a hand towards the kitchen. 'Don't forget there's a pav in the fridge and hot tea on the stove. Not that you'll find much milk, he didn't deliver again this morning.' She passed Rhiannon a glass. 'Drink this hot toddy. It'll warm you up.'

'Thanks, May.' Rhiannon leaned over and kissed the other woman on the cheek. 'Sure you don't want to stay and have a talk.'

'No, it's past midnight. I'm an old chook, I'm off to bed.'

'Night then.'

'Goodnight, May,' said Cameron, wondering if he should say something like he'd be off home soon. But why say that? He'd sit in front of the fire and talk to Rhiannon until the sun came up if he could. That way, he could keep her safe. And if she enjoyed a rum toddy with him, all the better.

'Are you sure you don't want to take a shower,' she asked as May left, perching on the arm of a chair and sipping her rum.

'You two are determined to drown me. I've put up with a lot more than wet jeans in the army.'

'You're not in the army anymore.'

'You know, I could be forgiven for thinking you're trying to get me out of my pants.'

'Well, it's been a while.'

Before he could react to that, she laughed and raised her glass. 'I'd like to make a toast. To Suellen.'

He did the same. 'Suellen.'

They both drank some of May's rum concoction.

Eyes twinkling, Rhiannon raised her glass again. 'And baby ... whatever.'

Cameron raised his glass another couple of inches. 'Baby whatever.'

He watched her over the rim of his glass as they drank to Suellen's child. Clearly Rhiannon wanted to dwell on the positive aspects of the night, and he admired her for that.

Suddenly, she turned serious. 'You were a wonderful help tonight, Cameron. Thank you for not freaking out.' She gazed at the fire, a wistful expression on her face. 'I always find it emotional helping mothers bring babies into the world. I miss it.'

She missed Sydney—that's what she was really saying. She missed working in a big hospital where the salary would be higher and her skills more utilized. She missed her *life* and all it encompassed. However much he hoped she might stay in Bindarra Creek, the reality was that Rhiannon's life was somewhere else.

She was a city girl, and he was a third generation grazier.

'I can understand you missing it. I feel privileged I was able to help.' The events of the night had brought them closer, and suddenly he wanted to be honest with her, the way she'd been with him.

'Usually, I'm standing over someone after I've taken their life,' he said quietly. 'It was awesome being there at the beginning for a change.'

'Oh, Cameron.' She reached for his hand and threaded her fingers through his. 'I can't imagine the things you've had to do.'

A surge of memories came rushing back at the sight of their entwined hands. Good memories, mostly of how they could talk, like this. And it hadn't been his intention to put a downer on the night, so he was grateful when she didn't say anything else, didn't ask him any probing questions he couldn't answer.

'I hope it wasn't too confronting for Suellen, having me there,' he said eventually.

'I think she was grateful. It will be all over town tomorrow that you were present at the birth.' She squeezed his hand. 'I wouldn't be surprised if she names the baby Cameron.'

'Oh, come *on*.' He smiled at her teasing. 'The locals will be taking bets on it.'

She laughed, then sat up like she'd suddenly remembered something. 'Are you hungry? I'm *starving*.'

'I'm not surprised. You only ate half your ribs.'

'Want some Pavlova?' She raised her eyebrows, looking like a teenager who'd just suggested they raid their parents' liquor cabinet.

He didn't want to let go of her hand but her infectious mood was contagious. 'I suppose you could twist my arm.'

She jumped up. 'Stay there. I'll get it.'

He looked up from stoking the fire when she came back a few minutes later. She was carrying a loaded tray complete with two servings of Pavlova, the bottle of Semillon they hadn't got around to drinking, and two wine glasses.

She put the tray on the coffee table. 'This will go well with the pav.'

He reached for the wine bottle, grateful it was a twist top and he didn't have to go into the kitchen in search of a cork screw. 'So, you have a sweet tooth after all.'

'Only sometimes.' She began eating the Pavlova, closing her eyes in appreciation as she swallowed. 'This is my favourite.'

He sipped his wine, watching as she polished off the entire plate of dessert. 'That delivery was intense. The adrenaline rush probably burnt off all your blood sugar.

'I feel better now.' Picking up the glass tumbler May had brought in, she sank down on the carpet and crossed her legs. 'My plan is to chase it down with this rum toddy, then follow it up with some of your wine. A successful birth deserves to be celebrated in style.'

He laughed. 'Can I join you down there?'

She tipped back her head and stared up at him. 'That was the intention.'

Warmth spread throughout Cameron's body, heating him more effectively than the fire. She shifted to make room for him and he levered himself down beside her. Holding the blanket around him like a poncho, he stretched out his leg and leaned back against an armchair.

'Comfortable?' she asked.

Cameron went all in. He wasn't a betting man but time was running out and he needed to do something to turn the odds in his favour. 'I'd be better if you came closer.'

She stared at him, brown eyes shining, the colour back in her face and lips.

He crooked an arm, blanket hanging from his shoulder like a cloak. Heat from the fire hit his chest. 'Come here.'

She closed the gap between them, sliding her arm around his bare waist and bringing her head down on his shoulder.

Cameron folded her in his arms and rested his cheek on her damp hair.

She sighed, soft body curled against him, all warm and fragrant from the shower.

Suddenly, Cameron couldn't breathe, like there was water in his lungs. 'Do you remember kissing me down the back of our property?'

'No.'

He blinked. *'No?'*

She raised her head and propped her chin on his chest, face radiant, soft eyes shining with amusement. 'Of course I remember. I often wonder whether it would be the same or different now we're older. I think about it every time I see you.'

He ran the pad of his thumb across her smooth cheek then slid his fingers under her hair to cup her nape. 'I think about it all the time.'

He kissed her, sensation spearing through his body at the first taste of her lips. He moved gently at first, lingering, caressing, greeting her in the manner in which he'd been dreaming. She tasted sweet, a mixture of milk and rum and heat so he had to physically hold himself back from going deeper, from coming on too strong, too soon.

He glided his lips over hers, teasing, tempting, his sole aim to give her pleasure, to make her want him the way he wanted her.

She raised her hands and shoved the blanket off his shoulders. Body trembling, she clung to him, soft breasts pressing against his bare chest, the brushed material of her tracksuit an excruciating barrier between them. He slipped a hand beneath her top and moved it in circles over her smooth back, body hardening to the point of pain when he discovered she wasn't wearing a bra underneath.

She whimpered, and Cameron's body roared to life like a high performance vehicle. He was in sweet Rhiannon heaven and he groaned against their fused lips, unwilling to break contact even for a second.

But a voice in the back of his mind reminded him they were in May's house and he would need to pull things back at some point.

Just not yet.

***

Rhiannon was floating.

Warm, strong hands roamed her back, kneading her muscles then gliding across her skin, stimulating every nerve, every pore, every hair follicle until the rest of her body craved the same attention. She'd been kissed before, but not like this, not in a way that heated her blood and made her head spin. And definitely not in a way that sent bolts of desire charging through her central nervous system and creating a direct path to her lower body.

She pressed herself against him, and he rewarded her by tightening his hold and deepening the kiss. She parted her lips, moaning her satisfaction at the increased pressure. All he'd done was kiss her and yet she was lost in a blur of sensation, of hands and tongues and a warm, rock hard body that smelled like a rainstorm.

Then suddenly he broke the kiss, nostrils flaring, chest rising and falling as he dragged oxygen into his lungs.

Rhiannon bent her head, hair falling across her face as she pressed her lips to his chest and trailed a line of kisses towards a flat, brown nipple.

Fingers plunged into her hair, thwarting her progress so she had no option but to lift her chin and look at him.

Face full of apology, he shook his head and glanced towards the door. 'May.'

Rhiannon crawled up his chest, pressed her lips to his and spoke against his mouth. 'May will be over the moon if she even suspects there's a chance of us getting together. Just look at the effort she put in tonight.'

He smiled, smouldering gaze dipping to her mouth. Then he wrapped his fingers around her wrist, raised it to his lips and pressed a kiss against her racing pulse. In that case, we really shouldn't disappoint her.'

CHAPTER FOURTEEN

Cameron slipped out of Rhiannon's warm bed around five the next morning. Careful not to wake her, he left the bedroom door ajar and stepped into the small living room where they'd discarded most of their clothes.

He groped around in the dark for his jeans and pulled them on, the denim scratchy and stiff from being soaked with rainwater. Knee cracking, he sat down on the small cream leather couch, wincing as he bent over to put on his socks and shoes. He was already paying the price for that bottle of Semillon they'd shared in bed. As he'd explained to Jed, his tolerance was way down after years in the SAS.

Thinking of Jed reminded him of home and he grabbed his phone off the lamp table where he'd left it after sending Tori a late text message. He'd explained that he'd had a few glasses of wine, had helped deliver a baby, got caught in the storm and had decided to stay at

Rhiannon's. He swiped his finger across the screen. Sure enough, she'd sent a reply.

Ooooooh!!! Don't do anything I wouldn't do. I'll let Dad know, if he asks.

The message was followed by a cute cartoon picture of two baby animals kissing and a red heart suspended above them.

Shaking his head, he looked around for his shirt and jacket. Damn! May had taken them into the laundry last night. She'd been going to put his shirt in the dryer. Perhaps she'd hung his jacket in there too. Cameron shivered as the frosty morning air hit his chest and back. After the rain had stopped in the early hours, the temperature had plummeted to around two degrees Celsius.

He went back to the bedroom door and opened it a few centimetres, greedy for one last look at the beautiful woman he'd made love to last night. Rhiannon was lying on her side, knees drawn up to waist level, one hand beneath the pillow, the other clasping the blanket under her chin like she was already missing his warmth. He smiled, hoping it was his love making that had left her in that deep, satisfied sleep.

Treading lightly, he crossed the living area and let himself out. In the hallway, he paused to switch on his torch app. Using the phone as a flashlight, he turned left and headed towards the rear of the house. To his way of thinking, May's bedroom would be situated at the front of the property like many homes built in that era. Despite Rhiannon's assurances that May was playing matchmaker, he didn't want to be caught doing the walk of shame at five in the morning.

On his right, a sturdy wooden door stood open. Cameron stuck his head inside and shone the beam around the room. It was the laundry. And there was his jacket, hanging from a wire hanger. The hanger was hooked over a pull-out indoor clothes line. Directly ahead was the clothes dryer, mounted on the far wall.

He slipped inside the room, slid his jacket off the hanger and shrugged it on. At the dryer, he shone his torch through the viewing pane and could see his shirt was inside.

Holding his phone between his teeth, he opened the door. The machine let out a loud beep and he froze, hoping the sound didn't disturb the sleeping women. Reaching into the dryer, he dragged out his shirt bringing with it a pair of bright red, racy knickers. He caught the knickers halfway to the floor and returned them to the dryer. There were at least five pairs of similar brightly coloured undies inside.

Very nice.

Smiling like a Cheshire cat, he took his phone from between his teeth and with his shirt clutched in one hand crept from the room.

Outside, he shone the torch around the outside of May's house. He was standing beneath some kind of lean-to or awning. Two of Rhiannon's uniforms hung drying on hangers out of the way of the rain. Lined up against the back wall of the house were a multitude of different sized pots housing every shade and variety of flowering Camellia japonica.

The light fell on a particularly healthy looking shrub, weighed down with large, deep pink blooms. They'd had that variety in their garden at Bindarra Downs when his mother was alive. She'd loved it. At this time of year she would fill the house with flowers. Everywhere you looked there were float bowls full of them. She used to say it was the hardiest flower for withstanding the frosty New England winters.

He'd forgotten that.

Cameron's heart cramped in his chest as he thought about Rhiannon again. She and Tori were already good friends and even Jed had begrudgingly admitted 'he liked the sassy young thing from the city'. But as a former nurse, his mother would have loved Rhiannon's dedication to her job, and the strength she'd displayed in fighting for it. Yes, somehow Cameron innately knew his mother would have approved of his choice.

He swallowed, his throat dry.

Is that what he'd done?

Chosen Rhiannon?

It hadn't taken long once he'd met her again, and many people said they'd known right from the beginning when they'd found their soul mate.

He leaned over and studied the blossoms again. Choosing the most perfectly shaped one, he snapped it off and put it in the pocket of one of Rhiannon's uniforms. Careful not to break the petals, he pushed it far enough down so it wouldn't blow out if the wind picked up, but left enough of the petals showing so the flower was clearly visible.

He'd call her later, now his head had caught up with his heart. He wanted to tell her how he felt about her and he needed to know if she felt the same about him. Words murmured in the heat of the night didn't count. He wanted to look at her in the cold light of day and admit to walking around Bindarra Creek at every opportunity in the hope of catching a mere glimpse of her.

Pleased with his handiwork, Cameron followed the line of pot plants to the end of the shaded area then turned down the side of the house. Branches from a neighbour's tree overhung the paling fence, brushing against his shoulder and showering his chest with droplets of chilly rainwater.

He paused at the corner of the house and killed the torchlight. Out on the street, the stormwater run-off could be heard gurgling in the drains. Beside him, water dripped from a rusty downpipe.

And there was something else.

Another presence.

Cameron let the shirt he was holding slip silently to the ground.

He could hear it, sense it, *smell* it.

He just couldn't see it.

A breath here, one there.

A soft scrape from the direction of the verandah.

Animal?

Intruder?

He turned his head a fraction and slid the phone into the pocket of his jeans.

What he'd give to have his night vision goggles now.

He scanned the area as best he could under the subdued street lighting. A little way up the road he spotted the Honda, its dark grey paintwork barely visible against the washed out colours of the dismal winter morning.

Hugging the wall of the house, Cameron moved with stealth, neither too fast nor too slow. He was trained for this, his hands steady, heart rate constant, injured leg a non-issue. He didn't look at the Honda, didn't search right or left, just kept his focus on the verandah where a soft, tearing sound was coming from.

He mounted the steps sideways, protecting his head and back should someone come at him from the street.

A dark figure squatted by the front door.

Whoever this bastard was, he intended harming Rhiannon!

The figure turned.

Cameron grasped the man by the shoulders and hurled him sideways, surprised at his lightness. Caught off balance, the intruder was spreadeagled on his back on the wooden floor before he knew Cameron was there.

Cameron stood with a foot on either side of the man's skinny body and wrenched on the cords attached to the hoodie he was wearing. The man struggled to sit up, the hood pulled tight so it almost covered his face.

Cameron planted his foot on the man's chest and pinned him with his weight. *'Who the fuck are you?'*

'Max.'

Max?

'Don't hurt me.'

Judging by his voice, Max was young.

And skinny.

Sixty kilos wringing wet skinny.

And he *was* wet. Covered in milk by the look of the empty carton lying beside him.

Cameron lifted his foot off Max's chest. 'Get up.'

When he didn't move, Cameron leaned down, grabbed the front of Max's hoodie and hauled him to his feet. 'What are you doing stealing milk from an elderly woman?'

'I'm sorry.'

Cameron kept a firm grip on Max, holding him upright when he stumbled sideways.

Max stared at him with unfocused eyes. 'I've been on the drink.'

'You don't say.'

'I'm a bit pissed.' Max raised his hands and tried loosening the hood that had been pulled in tight around his face. 'It was a huge night, man.' He slurred the words and Cameron leaned away from the alcohol fumes rising up from Max's body.

'I got the munchies, needed something on my stomach. I knew when I got home my mates would have knocked off all the milk and probably eaten my share of the food as well.'

'Where do you live?' Lights were beginning to come on from inside May's house.

Max pulled the hood back from his face. He had dark hair and looked about nineteen. He pointed to a white weatherboard house with two rubbish bins standing in the driveway. 'That one. I'll pay her back, or I'll go down to the supermarket and buy her a few cartons.'

'That you will.'

'Please, don't call the police.'

'The police have better things to do than worry about a young person stealing the neighbour's milk. Do it again and you'll have me to deal with.'

'Got it. Thanks. I won't.'

Cameron pointed to the Honda. 'Who drives that coupe?'

Max shrugged. 'No-one in our house. I've seen it there a few times. Weird how the guy just sits there, watchin'.'

'Is he in there now?' Cameron let go of Max. The shock had sobered him up.

'Yeah, I saw him as I walked past. He's asleep, I think. I thought he was one of those insurance guys they send around to catch people who've had a compensation payout. You know, the ones who've been paid for a bad back and then they catch them digging trenches?'

The front door opened and May and Rhiannon peered out.

'Cameron, what's going on?' Rhiannon asked, her voice a little shaky.

'Stay there.' He turned and jogged down the steps to the front gate. Opening the latch, he headed for the grey Honda. Jaw set tight, anger burning in his chest, he jumped the gutter and approached the car on the driver's side.

Cameron flung the door open, reached into the car and pulled the keys from the ignition.

'What the hell?'

Stocky, fortyish, buzz cut.

'Get out!' Cameron grabbed the man's arm, hauling him up and out of the car. 'Who are you?'

'Who are *you*?'

'Someone you don't want to mess with.' Cameron got right up in the man's face. 'I know you're watching my girlfriend.'

'Cameron, what are you doing?'

He turned to see Rhiannon standing near the back of the car. She was barefoot and dressed in her grey tracksuit.

He pointed at the man. 'Is this him?'

She nodded.

'I wasn't going to hurt her.'

Cameron swung around. 'Why blind her with your high beam and follow her to the police station? And why are you parked here at five in the morning?'

Sweat broke out on the man's forehead and he licked his lips. 'She saw me in the servo and took off so fast I thought she was panicking. I put the high beam on her so I could keep an eye on her, make sure she didn't jump out of the car and run.'

'And at the police station?'

'I was trying to scare her off so she didn't report me.'

'Who sent you?'

Nothing.

'She's forwarded your details to Sydney. We'll find out anyway.'

Silence.

Cameron grabbed the back of the man's jacket, spun him around and shoved him across the bonnet of the car.

'Cameron, *please.*'

It was Rhiannon, a spark of anger in her voice.

Cameron turned to look at her. She was glaring at him, fists curled at her sides. At the front gate, May stood watching along with Max. A couple of Max's housemates had wandered out onto their front porch as though spectators at a football match. Across the road, lights were coming on as people wandered outside to see what was happening.

'We should find out exactly who he's working for, Rhiannon.'

'I have my suspicions, and this isn't a military interrogation.'

'No, it's your life!'

When she didn't say anything, he shook his head in disbelief then leaned over and growled in the man's ear. 'You're wasting your time. Get out of town now, you hear me, because there's nothing for you in Bindarra Creek. I catch you around these parts again, I won't be so friendly next time.'

The man nodded to show he understood.

Cameron went over to Rhiannon, watching as the man straightened up and got back in his car. 'Don't worry. He won't be bothering you again.'

Anger flashed in her eyes and she backed away from him, colour high in her face. 'What do you think you're doing?'

Cameron frowned. 'Getting rid of him. Isn't that what you wanted?'

'What I didn't want was you putting on a show for the neighbours.'

With that, she turned on her heel and ran back towards the house.

'Rhiannon!' Cameron started after her, then stopped. He would make sure the Honda left the street before he followed Rhiannon to find out why she was so upset with him. After all, it was obvious the man was up to no good.

When the Honda was out of sight, he strode back to May's house, ignoring the cheers from Max's mates who'd clearly been on a bender all night.

'Are you all right, Cam?' May asked, wringing her hands as he came in the gate.

'I'm fine, May. Don't worry.'

Max was openly staring at him, the beginnings of hero worship in his eyes. 'That was awesome, man. You're a real badass.'

'Max, why don't you go home and sleep it off?'

'Oh no, I'm going to cook him some bacon and eggs,' said May. 'The poor boy's so hungry he's been drinking my milk. Would you like some, Cam?'

Cameron jogged up the front steps. 'No thanks, May. I need to talk to Rhiannon.'

CHAPTER FIFTEEN

Cameron found Rhiannon in her bedroom. She was pulling up the bedclothes, movements quick and agitated. Refusing to meet his eyes, she smoothed out the sheets and hauled the blankets around like she was trying to cover up what happened last night.

He swallowed. 'Want to tell me what's going on?'

'This is exactly what I didn't want.' She picked up a pillow, fluffed it up then flung it down on the bed. 'You didn't listen to me.'

'What do you mean?'

They faced each other, the bed a gaping chasm between them.

'How long have I been in Bindarra Creek?'

Was this some kind of trick question? Rhiannon's lips were pulled into a thin line and her chest heaved with barely contained anger.

'I thought it was about a year.'

She nodded, back rigid, her normally warm, liquid eyes, cold and distant. 'That's right. A year. An entire year where I've been conscious of my every move.'

'You don't have to worry about that anymore, I got rid of the guy. I doubt he'll be back.'

'Oh, that's just great.' She gave a bitter laugh. 'You waltz into town, the big tough SAS guy and fix everything for me.'

Cameron narrowed his eyes. 'I didn't go looking for him. He was parked out the front.'

She sat down on the bed and hugged the pillow to her middle. 'For a whole year, I've been conscious of my every move, refusing to join a gym, refusing to go on dates, until last night ...'

She pressed her fingers into her temples. 'I shouldn't have asked you over here.'

Her words were like a fish hook in Cameron's stomach. 'You're regretting it already?'

She jumped up and spun around. 'You blew it, Cameron. My lawyer told me to be discreet, to avoid the kind of thing that happened out there, where someone could take a photo that could be used against me in court—that could show me in a poor light.'

She threw out an arm and pointed in the direction of the house next door. 'Those drunk kids. They were taking pictures of you strutting around with no shirt on and throwing that guy over the bonnet, like, like ... some kind of Rambo!'

'You didn't have any objections last night.' He closed his eyes, regretting the words the moment they were out of his mouth. 'And I told you to stay inside but you chose to ignore me.'

'I'm not one of your subordinates that you can order around. What did you expect me to do, stay inside when there was a fight on May's front verandah?'

'That was the kid next door stealing milk. For Christ sake, you didn't have to run down the street after me. Who knows what that bloke could have done? If you'd stayed inside you wouldn't be on someone's camera roll now.'

For long moments neither of them spoke.

'Rhiannon....'

'It's very important I win this case ... that I restore my reputation.'

'In my eyes your reputation was never compromised. Are you sure you're not more concerned with the views of those who helped tarnish your reputation in the first place—like the hospital administrators?'

'What if I am? I love working as a midwife, Cameron. That's what I do.'

'If you love babies so much why don't you have a few of your own?'

She stared at him open-mouthed, her expression changing to one of disbelief.

'I'm sorry. That was out of line.' Cameron dragged in an unsteady breath and raked a hand through his hair. He wanted to reach out to her but everything he said only seemed to make things worse. 'Maybe I should go.'

She gave a curt nod. 'Maybe you should.'

Despite the angry words, he didn't want to leave like this. He couldn't walk away without touching her, without re-establishing a connection in some small way.

He came around the bed and stood looking down at her. Not knowing what else to do, he leaned over and kissed the top of her head, murmured the words against her hair. 'You might have regrets about last night, Rhiannon, but I never will.'

***

Fifteen minutes later, Rhiannon stepped out of the shower and wrapped herself in her robe.

If Cameron had no regrets, why had she woken up to find him creeping out of the house at five in the morning? She'd been looking forward to them waking up together, her body curled into his side, her head on his shoulder.

It was Sunday after all.

But no. Instead of waking up all dreamy and cosy, she'd woken up to the commotion of him sorting out both the milk thief and the man with the buzz cut. And she wasn't sure how she felt about what he'd done to them. She knew he was a highly trained soldier but she'd never seen that side of him, all controlled aggression and bulging muscles.

The way he'd dealt with the man in the Honda had been both terrifying and impressive. What would it be like to have a man like Cameron always on your side? In your corner. A person you could count on.

When had she ever had that?

Sitting down on the bed, she buried her nose in the pillow and breathed in his scent.

She was so selfish!

She wanted it all.

She wanted Cameron, and she wanted to go back to Sydney too.

It was impossible.

Cameron loved Bindarra Downs. It was his home, and he would never leave. He belonged there. He was a man of duty, and his duty was to his ailing father and his teenage sister. He wasn't the type to walk out on his responsibilities and the ones he loved.

And if he falls in love with you, he won't walk out on you either.

But how could she be certain he *would* end up falling in love with her? After an incredible night, she'd woken up to find him gone without so much as a kiss or a short note.

It had hurt—so much that she'd already been feeling disappointed and angry when she'd opened the door to find him reading the riot act to a youth named Max.

Rhiannon groaned. How could something so beautiful go so wrong so quickly? If he'd just stayed in bed with her, the man in the Honda might have been gone by the time they'd woken up.

Her mobile phone rang and she jumped, the upbeat tempo of the Chilli Peppers 'Higher Ground' lifting her spirits.

It had to be Cameron. Who else would be calling early on a Sunday morning?

She snatched up her phone where she'd left it on the bedside table.

Richard Strong.

Rhiannon's hopes plummeted to earth like a shooting star.

Did the man never sleep?

'Hello Rick!'

'Sorry to call so early. Did you get my voice message?'

'No.'

'I left a message last night asking if you'd be able to come down to Sydney for a few days.'

Rhiannon frowned. There'd been three missed calls on her mobile. She'd assumed they'd all been from Suellen's mother.

'Anyway, it doesn't matter now,' Rick Strong was saying. 'We've had a big break. Dominic Mullen's entered rehab.'

CHAPTER SIXTEEN

Rhiannon stepped off the CountryLink Express at Sydney's Central Station and joined the throng of commuters leaving the platform. Office workers zigzagged in and around ambling tourists, leather satchels slung diagonally across their chests, styrofoam cups clutched in one hand, mobile phones in the other.

Heart fluttering like she'd consumed too much caffeine, Rhiannon made the connection to the city circle line and ten minutes later exited Museum Station. The offices of Richard Strong & Co. were located in Sydney's legal precinct, close to the Supreme Court of New South Wales.

In the foyer, she took the crowded elevator to level 25, watching as office workers made their escape at every floor, seemingly relieved to have made the journey without the obligation to speak to anyone.

In the familiar waiting room of Rick Strong's office, his young receptionist was working her way through a pile of mail, letter opener in hand.

Hands clammy, Rhiannon searched her mind for the girl's name.

'Hello, Ms. Scott.'

'Morning. How are you?'

'Well, thanks. I'll just let Mr. Strong know ...'

'Rhiannon, come through.'

Rhiannon turned to see Rick standing in the doorway to the conference room. Trim in an expensive business suit and co-ordinated shirt and tie that would make a newsreader proud, he wore gold-rimmed glasses and a confident expression.

'Thanks for making the trip on such short notice.'

'It was helpful you called on a Sunday. It gave me time to clear my leave with Doctor Warner.' Hopefully, the time away from Bindarra Creek would clear her head about Cameron as well.

'How was the drive down?'

'I only drove as far as Armidale. From there I caught the train.'

'That's a relaxing way to do it.'

Too much time to stare out of the window and brood, she thought, taking a seat at the conference table. She'd been trying to concentrate on all the positives if Rick Strong settled the case, but her mind kept sabotaging her, reminding her of everything she stood to lose if she left Bindarra Creek.

'How's things?' asked Rick.

'Pretty much the same.'

That was a lie. Her life had turned upside down since Cameron Reid arrived home. 'I shouldn't have any more problems with the guy who's been following me. A friend confronted him, not that he told us who he was. There was a bit of a commotion.'

'I haven't received any info back about that number plate.' Rick pulled her file towards him. 'It doesn't matter now. Dominic Mullen's desperate to settle.'

'What changed his mind all of a sudden?'

'His wife came forward and admitted she's been protecting him.' Rick rolled his eyes. 'As if. Protecting the house on the harbour and the Benz more like it.'

'Why now?'

'Their fourteen-year-old son began raiding his father's stash and dealing it at his swanky boarding school. Mum freaked out when she got a call from the principal. Broke down apparently. She's terrified the son's taking after his old man.'

Rick rested his elbows on the conference table and steepled his fingers. 'Mullen's lawyers have had a hotline to this office wanting to settle. They're desperate to keep it out of court and out of the press. That puts us in a very strong position.'

Rhiannon waited for the euphoria to hit, the unbridled excitement at the prospect of regaining her job, her life. But all she felt was relief that the court case wasn't going to eventuate. That she'd avoid having her face splashed all over the media.

'Okay. What happens now?'

'I've negotiated a settlement figure which I hope will be acceptable to you. It will have to remain confidential of course.'

Rhiannon nodded.

He stated a figure.

Rhiannon's mouth fell open. With that kind of money she could afford to buy a home in Bindarra Creek.

Bindarra Creek?

Why had her first thought been of Bindarra Creek? Why not a deposit on a property in Sydney?

'Are you happy with that?'

She closed her mouth and nodded. 'Just a bit stunned, that's all.'

'Sure, I understand, it's come out of the blue. Dr. Mullen will be required to pay your legal fees and sign a Statutory Declaration stating his accusation against you was false. That will take care of the unfair dismissal case at the hospital.'

'That's the most important thing to me, the retraction in writing.'

'I know, but I'm determined to get you proper compensation as well. The hospital will have to reimburse you for lost wages and I'm seeking to recover your relocation costs as well. And then there's the emotional cost ...'

Rhiannon waved a hand. 'Oh really, I'm fine ...'

'No Rhiannon, that was a huge demotion, having to leave the city because they rendered you unemployable.' Rick was getting worked up now, indignant on her behalf.

'It hasn't been that bad.'

'But it could have been.'

She supposed so. She'd surprised herself with how well she'd coped. Now she knew what people meant when they said you don't know your inner strength until you've truly been tested.

Rhiannon watched as Rick began searching through her file for some document or other. She appreciated her lawyer's passion. He would have been formidable in court if the case had made it that far.

Not that she was complaining.

She couldn't believe it was almost over.

'This has all happened very quickly and it's important we move fast. That's why I asked you to come down. If you're satisfied, I can draft a Deed of Settlement now and have it delivered to Mullen's lawyers for signing. If I can get you back in to sign after lunch we can have it all wrapped up and filed at the court this afternoon.'

Rhiannon nodded. 'That would be fantastic. I've arranged to have lunch with my parents in the city.'

'Oh, nice. How about I message you when we've received the signed documents? You can call in any time after that. I'll be here.'

Rhiannon smiled. 'I'll keep an eye on my phone.'

They stood up and walked together towards the waiting room. 'Are you staying with your parents?'

Rhiannon shook her head and glanced sideways at Rick Strong. 'I booked into a hotel close by. Things are still a bit strained between Dad and me.'

'He hasn't come around yet, after almost a year?'

'No. He still believes I shouldn't have sued the hospital and Dr. Mullen.'

'I can't understand it. I know the medical profession have a tendency to close ranks but your father's reaction does surprise me.'

'Someone had to take a stand and force them to face the issue, otherwise patients would have been at risk.'

'You've been brave throughout all this, Rhiannon. It's been a very unsavoury business.'

Sudden tears pricked the backs of Rhiannon's eyes as they halted at the end of the corridor. She'd gotten to know Rick Strong fairly well over the past year. He'd made himself available whenever she'd needed him, answering all of her questions no matter how trivial, and using layman's terms which she always appreciated. Rick Strong had lived up to his name, exceeding every expectation she'd had in a lawyer.

Rick Strong believed in her.

So did Cameron. He'd accepted everything she'd told him the other night without question.

In my eyes, your reputation has never been tarnished.

'This victory is as much yours as it is mine, Rick. I couldn't have done it without you.'

'Thanks, Rhiannon.' He put a light hand between her shoulder blades, a friendly touch, nothing more. 'It's not over yet but we're damn close. And I'm just doing my job.'

'Well, don't forget to spend some time with your family. I've been getting phone calls and emails from you at all hours of the morning, seven days a week.'

He smiled like it was no big deal and changed the subject. 'What's on the agenda apart from lunch?'

'I was thinking of going out to the hospital.' She'd been toying with the idea of visiting her old colleagues. And she'd been wondering what it would be like to walk through the front doors again, to visit the birthing suite and neo-natal wards.

'Do you think you'll go back and work there?' Rick leaned against the wall, arms folded like he had all day when she knew he didn't.

'I don't know. I thought it might help me come to a decision.'

'You might like to know that since Mullen's confession others at the hospital have come forward.'

A chill slithered down Rhiannon's spine. 'Really? I wonder if I know any of them.'

Rick straightened up and put his hands in his trouser pockets. 'I'm sure you would. Mullen arranged to have some of them fired. Others were threatened with dismissal when they raised their concerns about his health, so they kept quiet.'

'I thought I was the first.'

'It appears not.'

Rhiannon massaged her temples in an effort to ease the sudden pressure. 'So, any of these people could have chosen to come forward and validate my story but they chose not to?'

'I'm afraid so.'

She thought about her many Bindarra Creek friends. May, Doc. Warner, Tori, Jed, Suellen, Kevin Strickland

and the ladies on the CWA. They would never have abandoned her like that. 'That is so gutless.'

Rick nodded. 'The only good thing is, it strengthened our case.'

Rhiannon took a deep breath and straightened her shoulders. How could she go back and work among staff who'd known she'd been telling the truth and had chosen to remain silent? How could she ever look upon them the same way? How could she trust them?

Dominic Mullen's false accusation might have resulted in her losing her job and her reputation being ruined.

But she hadn't lost her life.

She might have even found it.

CHAPTER SEVENTEEN

'Your look well, sweetheart.' Monica Scott turned to her husband Robert. 'Doesn't she, Rob?'

'Hmm.' Robert Scott continued to study the menu. 'Must be the country air.'

Rhiannon looked around the French café with its hanging lanterns and blue striped, scalloped awnings and attempted to make conversation. Outside the window, trains rushed past in a blur on route to Circular Quay Station, glimpses of the bridge and sparkling harbour visible in the near distance.

'This place has a bit of atmosphere, Mum.'

'The food's beautiful. I often come here with the school's fundraising mothers.'

Rhiannon smiled a little. 'I left school fourteen years ago, Mum. Shouldn't you be done with the fundraising committee?'

'She loves organising functions and they always need people,' said her father, closing the menu and putting it on the table. 'I think I'll have the pork belly.'

'That sounds nice,' said her mother. 'I might order the same.'

'Pork belly's on the fatty side.' Robert Scott looked his wife up and down. 'Maybe you should have the salad.'

Rhiannon glared at her father and spoke in a cold voice. 'Make sure you're not being taken for granted, Mum—and order what you want.'

Her mother's face turned bright red and she began consulting the menu for a second time. Robert Scott turned away and began checking out the other diners.

Rhiannon picked up her water glass and took a long drink, hoping the ice would cool her temper as well as her mouth. She'd spent the last couple of hours wandering through the shops in the Pitt Street Mall and choosing a few nice outfits for summer. After that, she'd walked through the Botanic Gardens, mentally gearing herself up for the meeting with her father. She'd been hoping to stay calm in light of his chauvinistic attitudes but twenty minutes in and she'd already worked up a full head of steam.

'I'll have the smoked salmon salad.' Her mother closed the menu and smiled at Rhiannon. 'That's fantastic news about the case being settled, sweetheart. Who would have thought the wife would come forward.'

Rhiannon's head began to ache. 'Why is it so hard to believe that she'd seek a formal intervention?'

Flustered, Monica Scott glanced at her husband 'Well, because it's her husband.'

'Loyalty is an admirable quality, Mum, one of the best, but you can be loyal to a fault. Dominic needed someone to intervene. He was in total denial. This way, he'll get the help he needs.'

'So when are you moving back?' asked her father.

'I haven't decided. I've been thinking there's no rush for me to come home. There are a few things that need to be sorted out in Bindarra Creek.'

Suddenly, the weight lifted from her shoulders, as if speaking the words aloud reaffirmed in her mind the action she needed to take.

Her mother's face fell. 'Do you think there's a chance you will stay there?'

'There's a chance, Mum,' she said gently. 'I need a bit more time to see a few things through. And if I do decide to come home, I want to make sure Dr. Warner has another nurse to take over. It's hard to entice medical workers to the country.'

But she had time on her side. With the case settled she could stay on in Bindarra Creek and see if things worked out with Cameron. She'd sent him a text letting him know she'd been summoned to Sydney by her lawyer. His reply had been swift and straight to the point just like the man himself.

Thanks for letting me know. Take care. C.

Suddenly, she couldn't wait to get back.

'You know, you can always come up and visit,' she said. 'There's a lovely bed and breakfast called Fig Tree

Lodge where you could stay. There's also some amazing wineries in the New England area.'

'I'd like that,' her mother said.

'So, you're going to drop out of the mainstream and stay out in the sticks?' asked her father.

'It's not the sticks, Dad. You make it sound like I'm joining a commune. The people are hard-working country people. You haven't even been there.'

And you didn't come up fifteen years ago when I won the junior tennis championship either.

It had been Cameron who'd comforted her that day. He'd told her not to worry, that despite her father promising he'd make the trip there would be a good reason why he'd missed her final match. But her father hadn't called, and when she'd trudged off the bus the following day with all the other billets, trophy in hand, it had been her mother waiting to collect her with an apologetic smile and an excuse for her father.

'She's right, Rob,' her mother was saying. 'You shouldn't criticise the place when you haven't even been there.'

'I don't *need* to go there to know what it's like.'

For the first time in her life, Rhiannon saw her father for what he was. 'You know, Dad, you have little insight and you're a man with a very big ego.'

She gathered up her things, pushed back her chair and stood up. 'I'm sorry, Mum.'

Packages in hand, she brushed past the other diners on her way to the front door. She'd have to arrange to meet up with her mother another day, on her own.

Monica Scott caught up with her in the lobby.

'Rhiannon! Wait!'

Rhiannon turned and walked straight into her mother's arms. 'I'm sorry, Mum, I can't talk to him. I try, but it's always the same. Maybe we're too alike.'

Her mother made a scoffing sound then held her at arm's length. 'You're nothing like your father. And you're right, he *is* a man with a very big ego. When people enquire about you, he wants to say you're working in some big, prestigious hospital. Admitting you're a general nurse in a country doctor's surgery isn't good enough.'

'Well, that's his problem,' Rhiannon mumbled, gripping both her mother's hands and giving her a watery smile. 'I know better now, thanks to the people in Bindarra Creek.'

Her mother put an arm around her waist and they walked a little way towards the front of the building, keeping out of the way of the foot traffic. 'You have to know he's not all bad, sweetheart. He does care in his own funny way.'

'Gees, Mum, you could have fooled me.'

'He might not have been up to Bindarra Creek himself, but he ... arranged for someone else to go up.'

Rhiannon frowned.

What on earth was her mother talking about?

'He was worried that Dominic Mullen might send someone up there to put pressure on you to drop the case, like he did in the beginning, so ... now don't get mad ... he sent a man to keep a look out over you.'

Rhiannon froze. 'A *man*?'

Her mother nodded. 'He called some security firm.'

Speechless, Rhiannon stared at her mother. Had the stranger in the Honda, the man with the buzz cut been sent by her *father*?

'Is this for real?' Rhiannon clapped a hand to her forehead, the handles of the shopping bags sliding up to her elbow. 'Do you know what this guy looked like?'

Her mother shook her head. 'I've never seen him, but I know your father took a call from him yesterday. He said he'd been spotted and he thought it best he return to Sydney. He said if he didn't leave Bindarra Creek he was going to get reported to the police.'

'Oh. My. *God*.' Tears stung the backs of Rhiannon's eyes and she shook her head. Would she ever understand her father? 'Do you know how much worry that guy caused me? I assumed he was sent up by Dominic Mullen's legal team.'

Her mother laid a hand on her arm. Passers-by glanced sideways at them with interest. 'I know your father's a difficult man but don't be too hard on him. He's part of the medical establishment and he knows how they close ranks. He knew they'd kill your career, and that's exactly what happened.'

Rhiannon took a shaky breath. 'That's all very well, Mum, but how could I have lived with myself if something happened to a mother or a baby? The guilt would have eaten me up, it would have destroyed me.'

'I know, and I'm so proud of you.' Her mother sighed. 'So is your father, in his own strange way. He's the type of man who doesn't know how to show his feelings. It takes me a while but I know how to get around him.'

Doesn't know how to show his feelings?

For a former SAS officer Cameron certainly knew how to show his.

Her mother reached up and cupped her cheek, the way she used to do when she was a child. 'What I'd like you to do is to come inside, sit down and have lunch. And after you sign those documents this afternoon, come and stay with us for a couple of nights. We'd both really like that. Will you do that for me?'

Rhiannon bit down on her lip. So much had happened since early yesterday morning when Cameron had confronted the man with the buzz cut that her mind was reeling. But how could she refuse her mother? These were her parents and Rhiannon loved them. Her father could treat her mother a whole lot better than he did, but Monica Scott appeared a lot less troubled by that than her daughter.

She nodded. 'Okay, Mum. I'll come back inside and I'll come home for a few days. I'm due holiday leave, and Doc. Warner said I can take as long as I need to get things fixed up here.'

'Thank you, sweetheart.' Her mother wrapped her arms around her and gave her a fierce hug. Then she took half the shopping bags off Rhiannon and together they turned and walked back to the café. Ignoring the curious glances of the wait staff, and vowing to get through lunch without losing her temper with her father again, Rhiannon followed her mother back to the table.

She'd try and make peace with her father as best she could, for her mother's sake. After all, he'd cared enough to send the guy in the Honda to watch over her, even if Mr. Buzz Cut had scared her half to death in the process.

CHAPTER EIGHTEEN

'What are you doing moping out here on the verandah all by yourself?'

Tori sat down on the cane lounge beside Cameron, grabbed his beer from his hand and drank a few mouthfuls.

'Hey! You're not eighteen yet, and I'm not moping.'

'Yes, you are.'

'I'm admiring my week's labour.' While Rhiannon was away, he'd kept himself busy cleaning up the lawns and gardens around the homestead. Split rail fences had been repaired and painted white, the garden beds in the centre of the circular drive weeded and overturned. He'd even planted some new rose bushes.

'It's amazing the difference a tidy up can make. It's only cosmetic stuff, but it's beginning to look like home again.'

Tori leaned her head on his shoulder. 'It feels like home to me because you're back.'

Cameron smiled, his sister's words easing the ache in his chest. The hard work had kept him occupied, distracted him from thinking too much about Rhiannon and wondering if she intended coming back, or whether she'd only be returning to collect her things from May Bannister's house.

He'd received a second text message letting him know the case was settling and how relieved she was to be avoiding a hearing. She'd also told him the man in the Honda had been sent by her father to watch over her in the weeks leading up to the court case. The bloke had returned to Sydney after the altercation outside May's house.

Cameron shook his head and gazed at the grey and orange hues of the sky as the sun sank low over Bindarra Downs. Strange how some families worked.

Tori curled her hands and inspected her fingernails. 'Do you think Rhiannon will stay? A lot of people are going to miss her if she goes.'

'I'm hoping she'll stay, midget. I'm really hoping.'

'You like her, don't you?'

'Yep, I do.' Cameron more than liked Rhiannon. He loved her. It didn't matter that it had happened quickly.

He was sure.

He knew.

'She was a good tennis player when she was younger, midget. I first met her when we were fifteen. She was billeted at the Jacobs'. She hasn't told you this, but she met Mum. I brought her over here to see you when you were a baby.'

'Really?' Tori lifted her head from his shoulder so she could look at him. 'Why didn't she tell me?'

'She thought it would be odd with me away.'

'Yeah, I guess. I like her. I don't want her to go back to the city.'

Cameron put his arm around his sister's shoulders. It hurt to think Tori could lose another woman in her life.

He swallowed a mouthful of beer and searched for a more positive subject. 'It's great Dad's decided to go to Melbourne to get assessed.'

'I'm scared,' Tori admitted, all of a sudden looking like a little girl again. 'What if it goes wrong?'

'It's only to get assessed, he doesn't have to go through with it.'

'I know. And how good would it be if it worked?'

'He's definitely warming to the idea. I think he's been better this week since he made the decision to go.'

'Me too.' Tori smiled and looked over her shoulder to where they could see Jed through the window, setting the table. 'He's even cooking us a baked dinner tonight and one of those old-fashioned steamed puddings you love.'

'That was Mum's recipe and her mother's before that. She used to make it all the time.'

'Did she?'

'Yup.'

Cameron gazed out over the property with a sense of satisfaction. Jed had made a decision about his health and since doing so had developed a more positive outlook on life. It was about time Cameron did the same. At the first opportunity, he'd talk to Rhiannon, ask her if they could keep on seeing each other, even if she returned to Sydney. With time, understanding and a lot of travelling on his part, maybe they could make it work.

As much as he dreaded her leaving, he had to be supportive of her returning to her former job if that's what she wanted. He was committed to his ailing father and his partly raised sister. Bindarra Downs in itself was a huge commitment. It wasn't as if he could offer Rhiannon a life of excitement on the property. He loved this life, but not everyone did.

There was a tap on the window.

They looked around to see Jed beckoning them inside.

'Come on, dinner's ready.' Cameron stood, put his hands above his head and stretched out his back. 'We should hit the hay early tonight, we've got a big day ahead of us tomorrow.'

'I can't wait.' Tori skipped ahead and opened the screen door. 'I get to see Ryan.'

Cameron halted. 'Ryan *Jacobs?*'

She nodded, eyes sparkling, a grin splitting her pretty face.

'I thought the family were away.'

'They are. Ryan's at uni in Armidale, silly. He's coming to the show.'

'I can't believe he's that old. You two used to play together when you were kids.'

'I know, and then when we were at school, we didn't speak for about three years.'

'And now he's hanging around again?'

'He's not hanging around. We always got on really well. He just went through that stage when it wasn't cool to be hanging out with girls three years younger.'

Cameron followed his sister down the hallway. 'Well, he'd better behave himself if he wants to hook up with my sister.'

'God, Cam, you sound just like Dad.'

The whine in Tori's voice had him grinning at Jed as they came into the dining room. Winding Tori up was one of their greatest mutual pleasures.

'Please, don't say anything like that if you see Ryan tomorrow. *Daaad ... tell him!*'

'I won't be there,' said Jed. 'It'll be too wet underfoot and I want to watch the Rabbitohs and Bulldogs game.'

Cameron sat down at the table. 'You're just scared of those CWA ladies, mate. Don't worry, I've got everything under control. They like me, especially Vera Wilson.' He winked at Tori, making her giggle.

'I hope for Lucille's sake the weather stays fine,' said Jed, reaching for the salt cellar. 'Wouldn't want the old girl getting bogged in one of those paddocks.'

'Yeah, don't worry about us,' quipped Tori.

'I won't.'

'It's not supposed to rain,' said Cameron. It had rained all week after last Saturday's massive storm, mostly overnight. The dams were practically full and the new spring grass had turned Bindarra Downs from a dry, strawy brown to a lush green.

Cameron picked up the gravy boat and poured it over the generous helping of lamb Jed had served onto his plate. The rain had brought confidence with it, and the outlook for farmers and graziers was suddenly looking a whole lot better. And there was a buzz in the township as well with a concentrated push for the revitalisation of Bindarra Creek.

Yes, things were definitely looking up.

Cameron put a forkful of lamb in his mouth and gazed at the faces of his father and sister.

If only Rhiannon were here, things would be perfect.

CHAPTER NINETEEN

Rhiannon pulled into the parking area outside the showground just after 2p.m. A parking attendant in an orange, high visibility vest and wielding a matching flag indicated she turn right. Five rows of parked cars later, another attendant waved her into a parking space.

The weather had delivered a blue bird day for the New England Regional Show and though a little sodden underfoot, the straw laid down by the grounds staff had soaked up much of the moisture.

Rhiannon locked her car, grateful she'd decided to go back to the granny flat after arriving in Armidale earlier. Her new white sundress with the coloured hearts scattered all over it and her cherry coloured Doc. Marten boots were more suited to the occasion than any of the outfits she'd taken to Sydney.

Rhiannon set off towards the entrance, earbuds in place, smiling every time she thought of the camellia she'd found in the pocket of her uniform. The unexpected gift could only have been left by Cameron. It was exactly the same camellia he'd given her fifteen years ago when he'd taken her riding at Bindarra Downs. His mother had vases and bowls filled with them throughout the house. When she was leaving, Cameron had plucked one from a float bowl and given it to her with a smile.

She'd carried it all the way home to Sydney in the bus.

Rhiannon curled her toes inside her Doc. Martens, excitement bubbling up inside her. Cameron hadn't sneaked out of her bedroom at 5a.m. last Sunday morning without a word or a soft kiss. He'd left a gift for her to find, an endearing little gesture that served as confirmation for the decision she'd already made.

Bindarra Creek was now her home!

She bought a ticket and entered the showground through a set of old-fashioned turnstiles. Inside, caravans lined the roadway on both sides, vendors peddling everything from plastic bags stuffed with multi-coloured fairy floss, snow cones towering in cardboard cups and hot pluto pups on a stick. A little further on, more vans were stocked with kewpie dolls, kites and fluffy toys, and from the direction of the rides, girls screamed so loud Rhiannon could hear their shrieks over her music. Everywhere she looked, parents, children and groups of teenagers were laughing and joking, multiple showbags hooked over their arms.

Warm sun hit Rhiannon's skin and she breathed in the country air, pungent with a mix of farm animals, grass and hay. She wandered past a pavilion housing baby farm animals and another displaying the best of the region's fresh produce. Slipping on her sunglasses, she searched for the pavilion where the Country Women's Association were exhibiting their wares.

'Rhiannon!'

Rhiannon turned to see Tori standing a little way off, trendy in stretchy blue jeans and a pink halter top. She was smiling and holding hands with Ryan Jacobs.

'Hello.' Rhiannon grinned and pulled out her earbuds. She'd run into Ryan a few times since coming back to Bindarra Creek. 'Since when have you two been an item?'

'Since he came to visit his parents a few months ago and barely recognised the girl next door.'

Ryan blushed to the roots of his short cropped blonde hair. 'Can you blame me? She's changed a lot.'

'You'd changed a lot when I came back.' Rhiannon turned to Tori to explain. 'He was only four when I stayed with his family.'

'Hey.' Tori nudged Ryan with her elbow. 'Did you know Cam and Rhiannon hung out here when they were in high school?'

'No.'

'Neither did I. They have history, and they're keeping it from us.'

Rhiannon smiled, pleased Cameron had told Tori that they'd known each other back then, however briefly. Maybe one day, she'd tell Tori what she remembered of her mother.

But not today.

Today was for fun.

Rhiannon surveyed the crowded area. 'Do you know which pavilion the CWA ladies are in?'

'That one.' Tori pointed to a smaller pavilion set back a little from the others. 'Don't go over there now though, the parade's just about to start. Come on.' She grabbed Rhiannon's arm. 'Let's go watch.'

'I want to see May ...' And she wanted to find Cameron as well. She remembered he was going to check out some Angus steers and maybe some horses.

'You can see May later.' Tori tugged on her arm. 'Cam's driving Lucille in the Miss Showgirl contest.'

Rhiannon blinked. 'Is Lucille one of the entrants?'

Tori laughed and kept pulling her towards the parade ground. 'No, silly. Lucille's Cam's MGTD. She's a vintage roadster. Dad finished restoring her while Cam was away.'

Intrigued, Rhiannon followed along and soon they were climbing the steep stairs leading to the grandstand. On the far side of the oval, a gate stood open and Rhiannon could see a line of vintage cars ready to enter the arena.

'Dad was supposed to do it,' Tori said with a giggle. They sat down on a long bench and squeezed closer, making room for the crowd. 'But since he isn't allowed to drive, Cam had to step in.'

Behind the cover of her sunglasses, Rhiannon studied the line of cars until she located the shiny red convertible Tori was pointing to. It was third from the front and Cameron was sitting in the driver's seat, arm propped on the sill, trendy aviator sunglasses covering his eyes. A

191

blonde girl wearing a duck egg blue ball gown and white sash across her chest, was perched on the folded convertible soft top, dress skilfully arranged for maximum effect. She was talking to Cameron, and from time to time he'd turn his head and laugh at something she said.

Rhiannon's heart swelled in her chest until she could barely breathe. Cameron was a handsome, hometown hero, a decent, hardworking guy who'd left the army to take care of his family and Bindarra Downs. And take care of them he would. She'd already experienced his protective instincts when he'd flexed those big beautiful biceps and sent the guy in the Honda on his way.

His children too would know the protection of a loving father.

If you love babies so much why don't you have a few of your own?

Why *didn't* she?

Rhiannon felt a physical clenching in her womb.

She loved him, and she'd been right to come back here. She'd never been more certain of anything in her life.

The cars began rolling through the gates, moving at a snail's pace. Without picking up speed, they did a lap of the oval, showgirls smiling and waving in response to the cheering crowd. Rhiannon kept her eyes focused on Cameron, watching as he smiled and nodded every now and then to someone he recognised. One of them was Doc. Warner.

Then one by one the cars exited the arena.

'Come on. Let's go say hello,' said Tori. 'I want to get a photo of Cam and Louisa.'

'Louisa?' Rhiannon frowned. 'Louisa Porter, Suellen's sister?'

'Yes, Louisa was in Cam's car.'

Rhiannon thought back to the horrendous storm last weekend and Suellen's pre-mature labour. She'd noticed Louisa Porter's beauty that night but she hadn't realised it was the same girl in Cameron's car today.

'You go take your photo,' she said to Tori, suddenly reluctant to gate crash the pageant in her clumpy Doc. Martens. It wasn't the time or place to talk to Cameron and she'd be seeing him soon enough. She'd waited this long, she could wait a little longer.

'I didn't want to ask because I wasn't sure I'd like the answer,' said Tori. 'Do you have to go back to Sydney?'

Rhiannon shook her head. 'No. I'll be staying on as Doc. Warner's nurse for the foreseeable future.'

Tori threw her arms around Rhiannon and squeezed hard until Rhiannon yelped in protest.

'I'm so happy,' Tori said, grabbing Ryan's hand and dragging him off in the direction of the vintage cars. 'I can't wait to tell Cam.'

'Could you let me do it?' Rhiannon called after her. 'Please, Tori?'

'Oh, sure.' Tori turned and gave her a conspiratorial wink. 'My lips are sealed.'

As Tori dashed off in the other direction, Ryan in tow, Rhiannon made her way towards the pavilion. At the entrance, she ran into Kevin Strickland.

'Afternoon Rhiannon. Good to see you back in town and trying to dress like a local.'

Rhiannon looked down at her dress. 'What do you mean, Principal Strickland, I'm a country girl.'

He grinned. 'The red Doc. Martens. They're a bit too fashionable. Only wear the black ones out here.'

Rhiannon laughed. 'Failed again.'

'You can't help being from the city.'

'All packed for India?'

'Just about there.'

'Well, have a great time if I don't see you before you leave.'

'I'll be trying my hardest.'

She began to move inside when a deep voice spoke her name.

She turned, hands clammy, legs turning weak. Cameron was standing right behind her, dark hair brushed up at the front in the current style, black aviators perched on his perfectly proportioned nose. He was wearing a collared shirt in a royal blue colour that May would have approved of, grey loose fitting jeans that still managed to showcase a sensational pair of powerful thighs, and riding boots. Large riding boots.

'Oh, hi!' Rhiannon brushed her hair out of her eyes and tried not to dwell on the magnificent physique she knew lay under his fashionable country wear. 'I didn't expect to run into you here. I just saw you in the ...'

He whipped off his sunglasses and slid them into his shirt pocket. 'Parade?'

'Yes, the parade. You were driving Suellen's sister, Louisa.'

He nodded, eyes skimming over her white sundress. He smiled, a gentle curving of his lips. 'So, you're back?'

'Yes.' She hooked a thumb towards the door. 'I was just heading in to see May.'

'Me too.'

'Oh?'

'I wanted to buy something for Suellen's baby.'

'Oh, that's nice.'

She stared at him in dismay. Could they be any more awkward with each other? It had only been a week but she was so nervous she couldn't string two words together.

'Well, let's go in ...'

A warm hand clamped around her upper arm. 'Come with me.'

He steered her back the way she'd come, weaving through the crowd until they reached sideshow alley. Children were feeding ping pong balls into the mouths of grinning clowns while others threw darts at numbered balloons in a quest to win a fluffy animal to take home.

Rhiannon shook her head at a woman who was holding up a ping pong ball and beckoning her over. 'I could never win any of those fluffy animals.'

Cameron stopped walking and looked down at her. 'Which one would you like?'

'Sorry?'

He let go of her arm and walked over to the shooting gallery. She followed, watching as he handed over enough cash for one game.

'If we're going to talk fluffy toys before we talk about us, Rhiannon, so be it. Which one would you like?'

Talk about us?

She liked the sound of that.

He grabbed a rifle as casually as though it were a fishing rod. She knew the gun was harmless, but she suspected he'd handle a real firearm in a similar way. 'I bet you're a crack shot, Cameron Reid. You're looking very confident.'

He gave her a lopsided grin and hoisted the rifle onto his shoulder. 'Had to get your attention some way.'

'You got it!' She smiled, happy their easy-going rapport was back, the fight outside May's house forgotten.

People gathered around and she could hear murmurs of 'It's Cam', 'Cam's going to shoot' and 'Watch this.'

'You look beautiful in that dress, Rhiannon.' His heated gaze slipped over her. 'Are you going to tell me which one you want?'

Rhiannon's heart pumped, excitement fizzing through her central nervous system until every cell in her body was energised. She pointed to the panda sitting right on top of the pile. 'Pandas are my favourite, and that one is jolly and large and has a friendly face.'

'Fair enough. The panda it is.'

Without another word, Cameron closed one eye, aimed the rifle and with a repetitive flick of his wonderful wrist flattened every single moving duck with deadly precision.

Rhiannon gasped.

People behind clapped.

While the vendor used a stick to hook the panda, Rhiannon stared at Cameron in open admiration. 'That was impressive, soldier.'

'Enough to earn me a kiss?'

'Yes!' She flung her arms around his neck and pressed her lips to his warm, firm ones. He held her lightly by the waist, stubble grazing her cheek as people behind cheered.

They pulled apart and then Cameron was putting the panda in her arms.

Rhiannon laughed. 'Oh my God, thank you. It's enormous.'

'On second thoughts, I'd better carry it.' He took it from her again and she could tell from the expression on his face he was pleased he'd made her happy. 'You can't see over the top of it. You'll fall in the mud.'

'Perhaps we should put it in my car.'

'Good idea.'

Rhiannon told him which bay she was parked in and they headed in that direction, Cameron with the enormous panda tucked under his arm.

'You have an unfair advantage, being in the army.'

'I learned to shoot way before then. On the property, there's everything from rabbits to wild pigs.'

'Really?'

He nodded. 'I was recruited into the army because of my shooting.'

She hadn't known that, but how could she when they'd never been able to talk specifics about his time in the elite SAS.

'Well, my panda is much cuter than any wabbit or wild pig.'

He laughed and hitched the panda higher on his hip. 'Where are you going to put him?'

'On my bed, of course.'

'Lucky panda.'

At the mention of bed the air became charged with electricity. Suddenly, Cameron's expression turned serious.

'How was Sydney?'

'Tiring.'

That wasn't entirely true. Only with him did she feel truly energised. 'It's not the utopia I once thought it to be.'

'Get everything sorted out?'

She nodded. 'It's all settled. You'll be pleased to know that despite my fears I escaped with my reputation restored.'

'Somehow, I think your reputation would have been enhanced rather than restored.'

'That's a lovely thing to say, Cameron.'

He shrugged. 'It's true. You could have gone to the press in the beginning and accused him of being an addict. The current affairs programs would have been all over it like a pack of vultures. But you resisted the temptation to hit out and drag his name through the mud. You defended yourself, but you went through the correct channels to do it. It's admirable.'

Rhiannon bit down on her bottom lip in an effort to stop it trembling.

How did he do that?

More than anyone else in the world, how did he just 'get her' like that?

She glanced up at him, a pulse fluttering at the base of her throat at the hunger in his eyes. 'Thank you.'

He raked a hand through his hair and appeared to come to a decision. 'Why don't we just get down to the nitty gritty, Rhiannon? We're both thirty, and I don't know about you but I'm too old to play games. I think you know there's only one important question I really want to ask you.'

Was she staying in Bindarra Creek?

'The answer's yes, Cameron.' She reached up and cupped his cheek, his jaw rough in her palm. 'I love you, and I belong here, in Bindarra Creek. It's that simple.'

The panda hit the ground and the next instant she was swept into his arms and swung round and round.

Shrieking, she wrapped her arms around his sensationally wide shoulders and pressed her face into his neck, laughing as he let out a loud whoop.

'What's going on over there?' called a guy in an Akubra who was just about to get into his car.

'We're getting married,' Cameron shouted. 'Come over and be the first to congratulate us.'

Rhiannon lifted her head. *'Married?'*

Cameron's smile faded like the sun retreating behind a cloud.

'I ... I ... meant, yes I was coming back to live in Bindarra Creek.'

He set her on her feet beside the panda, and for a few awful moments Rhiannon thought he was going to turn on his heel and walk away.

'You ... you want to marry me?' she whispered.

He swallowed, Adam's apple bobbing in this throat. 'I thought I made that pretty clear.'

'I'm sorry I pre-empted the question. I've been so nervous thinking about seeing you again, and then I saw you driving Louisa.'

'There's nothing between me and Louisa.'

'I know.' Rhiannon smiled, joy welling up inside her as it finally sank in that he really wanted to marry her. 'I think I'm in shock.'

He came slowly towards her again, bluey grey eyes glittering in the sunlight. 'Well, you're the nurse but I could always check you over if you want?'

This time she didn't try to stem the tears that seeped from the corners of her eyes and ran down her cheeks. They would have children and they'd all live together with Jed and Tori at Bindarra Downs. A life laden with possibilities stretched before her. Maybe they would have horses again, maybe her parents would even come and visit. Maybe her father would mellow once he had grandchildren in his life.

'I've been worried all week you wouldn't come back,' he said in a choked voice. 'I hated the way we parted after that fight.'

'But we love each other, right? We don't stay angry for long. You taught me that.'

'I made a promise to myself that if you came back I was going to ask you to marry me.'

She swiped at the tears with the backs of her hands. 'I can't believe it.'

'Believe it! I *love you,* Rhiannon.' He raised his hands to cup her face and wipe the tears away with his thumbs. 'I'm a soldier and nothing much fazes me, but taking off my pants so you could get to that tick had me shaking in my boots. I knew then that I loved you.'

Rhiannon smiled through her tears.

He put his face close to hers and whispered in her ear. 'Does this mean the answer's yes?'

'Yes.' She clutched at his shirt to steady herself as he lowered his head and kissed her.

Warm lips covered hers in the most reverent of kisses, like he was making his vows right there and then.

Rhiannon wound her arms around his neck, pulled him close and kissed him with all of her being.

She was going to marry the love of her life.

She was going to marry Cameron Reid!

'There you are!'

They pulled apart and turned at the sound of May's voice. She was weaving her way through the parked cars, boots clogged with mud.

'May!' they cried in unison.

'Tori told me you were back. I waited and waited for you to come into the pavilion, and when you still didn't come I decided to bloody well find you myself.'

Cameron pointed to May, stopping her in her tracks. 'Don't come any further, May. The mud's worse down here and we're coming back as soon as we put this panda in the car.'

'Well, from what I could see there was a lot more going on than that. The panda's in the mud.'

They looked at the ground and started to laugh. The giant panda was certainly more black than white.

Deliriously happy, Rhiannon stood on tiptoes and kissed Cameron once again.

'Yes.' She murmured against his mouth, just so he knew she was certain.

The End

Thank you so much for taking the time to read my story *Shadows of the Heart* which is part of the **Bindarra Creek Romance Series**.

All reviews are appreciated.

A little about the **Bindarra Creek Romance series**:
13 months. 13 authors. 13 romances.

Welcome to Bindarra Creek, a struggling country town where people work hard and love deeply. Set in the picturesque tablelands of New England, Australia, Bindarra Creek is a fictional, drought stricken community full of intrigue, adventure, drama and romance.

Life and love in a small country town has never been more challenging.

~

Books in the Bindarra Creek Romance series:

Bindarra Creek Makeover - S. E. Gilchrist
Shadows of the Heart - Lee Christine
Second Chance Love - Susanne Bellamy
The CEO Mechanic - Sandie James
Reach for the Stars - Kerrie Paterson
Home to Bindarra Creek - Juanita Kees
Stolen Sanctuary - Stacey Nash
Tempting Fate - Erin Moira O'Hara
One More Day - Linda Charles
The Vine - Lauren K. McKellar
The Ghost of His Past - Simone Angela
Joanie's Dilemma - Marianne Theresa
Buckley's Chance - Noelle Clark

For more info on the other stories in this series, please visit

www.bindarracreekromance.com

OTHER NOVELS BY LEE CHRISTINE

In Safe Hands

In Safe Arms

In Safe Keeping

A Dangerous Arrangement

BIO

As a teenager Lee loved playing the guitar and writing songs. Those lyrics were all about love so when she turned her hand to writing novels later in life romance was the obvious choice. After her first two novels were relegated to a desk drawer, her third novel 'In Safe Hands' won the Romance Writer's of America Silicon Valley Gotcha Contest, the RWA Smoky Mountains Laurie Award and the RWA East Texas Southern Heat contest for best romantic suspense. In 2012, Escape Publishing chose 'In Safe Hands' as one of five launch titles.

Two more novels followed, 'In Safe Arms' and 'In Safe Keeping'. All three books can be read as stand-alones or as part of a series. 'A Dangerous Arrangement', book one in Lee's next romantic suspense series was released in June, 2015.

Lee's novels are sexy, fast-paced and contemporary. She lives on Australia's eastern seaboard and loves snow skiing and playing the alto saxophone.

Lee Christine is published with Escape Publishing and is an indie author

*

Reviews can help readers find books and increase a writer's visibility. I am grateful for all honest reviews. Thank you to any who have the time to let others know what you've read and what you thought of the book.

If you'd like to know more about me or would like to connect on-line, please visit the following links:-

www.leechristine.com.au

https://www.facebook.com/leechristine59

https://www.pinterest.com/leechristine59/

My twitter handle is @leechristine59

I'd love to hear from you!